THE
PERFECT
PROPOSAL

Sophie King

Neighbours ® FremantleMedia Australia Pty Ltd

www.neighbours.com

This novelisation © Sophie King 2018

Published 2018 by Corazon Books
(Wyndham Media Ltd)
27, Old Gloucester Street, London WC1N 3AX

www.corazonbooks.com

ISBN: 978-1-909752-32-0

Cover illustration © Patrick Knowles

For Richard

One

GAIL

The red dress or the blue? Or maybe a jacket and a skirt? Smart trousers perhaps? Gail gazed despairingly down at the pile of discarded outfits on the bedroom carpet. What exactly did a girl wear for a job at the prestigious Daniels Corporation? She glanced once more at the job advert which was lying on the bed next to her make-up bag.

WANTED: EXPERIENCED, AMBITIOUS, PROMOTIONS MANAGER WITH INITIATIVE.

How lucky that she'd spotted it. Something told Gail that this was exactly the job for her. Okay, so she might not be experienced in this particular line of work. But she could turn her hand to almost anything. She'd always had that 'I can do anything' attitude. Except perhaps when it came to mending a broken marriage …

Wasn't that why she needed this job so badly? That was the thing about divorce. Not only did it break your heart, it also broke the bank. If she didn't get something soon, she wouldn't be able to help out with next month's rent. Besides, she couldn't go on living at Dad's for ever … Of course, there was one little problem about the job, apart from the 'experienced' bit. She'd missed the application date for the interviews which were, according to the advert, being held today between 1 and 4 p.m.

'Just go along,' Dad had suggested. 'Turn up with your résumé and see if they'll still see you. What can you lose? At the worst, they might just turn you away.'

Even so, it felt a bit cheeky. Then again, 'Nothing ventured, nothing gained' as one of her old colleagues at the airline used to say.

'Come on,' Gail told herself. 'Stop having doubts and just get on with it. And wear the blue.'

Jeremy had always said the colour suited her …

Gail placed her hands on her hips and looked in the mirror. How exactly did she get here? Never, in a million years, would she have imagined that she'd be in this position now. A divorced woman, still in love – though God knows why – with her former no-good husband.

It didn't help that only this morning, a postcard had arrived in the post. It had a picture of a golden beach. On the other side, Jeremy had simply written, *'Remember this?'*

Of course she did. It was where they had spent their honeymoon. For a minute, Gail allowed herself to close her eyes and remember those idyllic days when they had stayed in bed, their arms wrapped round each other, staring out at the beautiful sea. If only she had known that not long afterwards, Jeremy would be seeing someone else on the quiet. In fact, not just someone. Several!

Over the years, she had lost count of the number of 'friendships' that her racing-driver husband had with other women. Yet there was always a plausible excuse for it. She was a work colleague. Or a woman in a shop who'd advised him on buying Gail some perfume. Or – once – a distant cousin. Why did men in glamorous professions always think they could get away with it?

Gail shook her head, rubbing her eyes as she sometimes did when she was tired or just a bit fed up. Damn. She'd gone and smudged her mascara. Now she'd have to put it on all over again. 'That's enough,' she said out loud, waggling a finger at the mirror image in front of her. 'You can send me all the postcards you want, Jeremy. And you can drive as many fast cars as you please. But it's over between us. Got it? Now get a move on, Gail. Or you'll be late for this interview which you don't even have!'

Was she making a stupid mistake? Despite that 'nothing ventured' determination, Gail couldn't help feeling very uneasy as she drove along the freeway towards the address on the advert. Perhaps this was just a waste of time. She could be at home, right now, applying for jobs that weren't past their deadline date. Yet nothing she had seen so far looked as interesting as this one.

Mind you, Gail thought as she took a right turn, she could do with a bit more information about the Daniels Corporation. After being out of town for so long, thanks to her job with the airline and then her marriage to Jeremy, she was a bit out of touch. All she'd been able to gather was that it was part of an international company run by someone called Rosemary Daniels who lived in the States, and its Australian interests were based in the Lassiters Complex, here in the Melbourne suburb of Erinsborough, which included the Lassiters Hotel, a coffee shop, The Waterhole pub, and other businesses.

Coincidentally, Dad's mechanics garage was also in the area. As she parked the car, Gail wondered whether she'd done the right thing in not mentioning this visit to him just in case it 'jinxed' it. She needed this job!

Gail's mouth went dry as she walked towards the reception. But despite her thumping heart, she made sure she was standing up straight with a broad smile. 'Always believe in yourself,' Jeremy used to say. 'If *you* don't, no one else will.'

Much as she hated to admit it, this was possibly one area where her ex was right.

'Hi,' she said confidently to the pretty young blonde woman on the desk who was wearing a *'Jane Harris: PA to Mr Robinson'* name badge. 'My name's Gail Lewis. I'm here for the promotions manager interview.'

Her pulse began to race as the woman looked down at a sheet of paper. 'We don't seem to have you on the list.'

Gail felt herself flushing. 'Well, Jane. It's like this. I only saw the advert this morning and, to be honest, it was too late to apply. So I thought I'd just turn up.' It was always important to address someone by their name. That had been part of her training too. It made that person feel special. She continued, 'I know that's a bit presumptuous but I've brought my résumé and I really think I could bring something to the job.'

It was the truth! Hadn't she learned from Jeremy that lying was wrong? But she could see this Jane hesitating. Any minute now and she'd surely be shown the door.

'It's very unusual but … well, as you're half an hour early, I'll have a word with my boss and see what he thinks.'

'I was early on purpose, actually.' Gail gave what she hoped was a winning smile. 'I have this thing about not being late.'

'Me too! Would you like to take a seat over there?' She indicated a sofa by the window.

'Thank you.'

Nervously, Gail sat on the edge, watching everyone go by outside the window. There was a distinct buzz in the air. Please make this work out! She began to feel excited – this was just the type of place she'd like to work in. Maybe she'd pay a quick visit to the Ladies to freshen up her lipstick.

'No! I don't believe it!'

There was a rather glamorous older woman by the washbasins, examining a large ladder in her tights. 'They're brand new. I've got a meeting in a moment. I can't possibly go in looking like this.'

Gail couldn't help but sympathise. 'I've got a spare pair in my bag somewhere. Here we are. I always carry one just in case.'

The older woman looked impressed. 'Me too. But I changed bags at the last minute. May I pay you for these?'

'Not at all. Happy to help.'

'Are you here for the interviews by any chance?'

'Yes. I am.'

The woman appeared to be appraising her coolly. 'Then good luck. And thanks once more for the tights. I'm going to put them on now.'

As she disappeared into one of the cubicles, a terrible thought struck Gail. Was that glamorous woman here for the same job as her? And if so, had she unwittingly helped a rival? How stupid of her!

Swiftly, Gail refreshed her lipstick and went back to the sofa. To calm her nerves, she reached over for one of the glossy magazines. Then she stopped. There, right in front of her, was a picture of Jeremy. *Her* Jeremy. It was an interview all about his career. Quickly, Gail scanned it. Did it mention the divorce?

But before she could read any more, Gail became aware of Jane the PA walking towards her. 'You're lucky. Mr Robinson has an unexpected gap. He will see you now.'

Reluctantly, Gail put down the magazine and followed the young woman across the shiny floor towards an open door. Her head was still whirling from the pictures she'd just seen. Such a shock! It was almost as if Jeremy had turned up in person – just at the very time when she needed to be cool, poised and able to talk herself into a job. In fact, she was amazed she'd got this far.

'Miss Lewis?' The man on the other side of the desk was looking at a sheet of paper in his hands. 'You're not on my list but my PA tells me that ...'

Then his face rose and met hers.

Gail heard him gasp just as she herself took in a sharp intake of breath.

'Paul?'

'Gail?'

'What are you doing here?'

'What are *you* doing here?'

'Is there a problem?'

This last remark came from Jane, who was looking distinctly worried, as if *she* had done something wrong, instead of Gail for walking in without an appointment.

'I wouldn't have applied for this position if I'd realised you were here.'

As soon as Gail said the words, she realised how rude they sounded. But it was too late to take them back. Besides, Paul was already speaking.

'And I wouldn't have agreed to take in a "walk-off-the-street" if I'd realised it was you.'

For a minute, they both stared at each other frostily.

'Would you like me to see Miss Lewis out?' suggested Jane.

Gail made to turn round. 'That might be just as well.'

But to her surprise, Paul shook his head. 'You're here now. And our airline days are a thing of the past. I've moved on.'

Gail looked around the smart office with its high-tech desk and reclining chair. 'So I see.'

'It would be good to catch up and find out exactly why you want this job.'

I *don't* now, Gail almost said. But somehow she kept her mouth shut. Of course she did. If she didn't find something soon, she wouldn't be able to help Dad out with the rent, let alone afford her own place.

'Great.' Jane sounded relieved. 'I'll bring in coffee then, shall I? How do you take it?'

'Milk with one sugar,' said Paul swiftly. 'If I recall correctly.'

'Actually,' cut in Gail, 'it's now black without any sugar at all.'

'Sounds like you've changed a bit. Why don't you sit down and bring me up to date?'

'Is this an interview or a friendly chat?'

'Let's call it both, shall we?'

Well, Gail told herself as she took a seat facing Paul's, here's another mess you've got yourself into. Try and get out of this one!

Two

PAUL

'Get a grip on yourself, man,' Paul told himself firmly. 'Just talk naturally.'

But it was tough. It had been such a surprise when Gail had walked into his office a few minutes ago. He just hadn't been prepared for it. It hadn't been a welcome surprise either. It reminded him of that brief fling they'd had. What a mistake that had been! The two of them were totally incompatible. And now, here they were, making polite conversation as though it had never happened. Of course, he couldn't possibly give her the job. Hadn't experience already shown that they wouldn't work well together? And besides, Gail had been his boss. She'd hardly take kindly to a reversal of roles. She might well question his orders and belittle his reputation with the other staff. God knows he'd worked hard enough to get to this position.

'So how long have you been working here, then?' asked Gail, crossing her legs in that way he remembered.

He used to swear she did it on purpose to show off her shapely calves.

Paul tried to sound more confident than he felt inside. 'Since I left the airline. It's a family business.'

She nodded. It was hard to tell whether she was impressed or whether she was thinking he was only there because of his connections. She'd be right on the last one. It was something which Paul was acutely aware of. When things got awkward, turn the tables on the other side. Hadn't he learnt that from his Aunt Rosemary? Perhaps he should do some probing himself and find out why Gail needed a job. After all, Jeremy Lord must bring enough money in. Or perhaps she was just bored.

But before he could ask, she got in first. Typical! 'You're probably wondering why I want a job so badly.' She sighed and uncrossed those legs again. Yet the wistful look in her eyes indicated she was doing this without thinking rather than trying to look attractive. 'The truth is that Jeremy and I have split up.'

'Really?' He hadn't expected that one.

Gail gave a sad smile. 'You clearly don't read the popular press. It was all over the front page – well, for a short time until they found someone else to write about.'

'I'm sorry.'

He meant it too.

'Is there any chance you two might get back together?' he added.

'Too late. We're just a statistic now. Another of those one in four marriages that ends in divorce.' She gave a rueful shrug. 'That's why I'm back to being a Lewis again – it felt more comfortable to return to my maiden name.'

For a minute, she looked as though she was going to

say more. Then she stopped. There was an awkward silence. It seemed too forward to ask why their marriage had ended, although Paul could guess. Hadn't there been rumours about Jeremy being a 'lady's man'? Maybe she'd booted him out. Or perhaps he'd left her for someone else.

'Can't be easy,' he said.

She gave a tight little nod. 'It's not. But you've got to move on, haven't you? That's what my dad is always saying. In fact, I'm staying with him right now. It's not exactly what I'd expected at my age but there you go.'

I didn't expect to be a widower, Paul almost said but managed to stop himself in time. They were here to talk about the job, weren't they? Not catch up on their pasts. 'Perhaps we'd better get down to practicalities,' he said, changing his tone to one which was more professional. 'I see you've brought your résumé with you.'

'Yes.' Gail sat up very straight as if remembering she was at an interview. 'I know I don't have the qualifications or experience you're looking for. But I'm able to turn my hand to most things and I'm not scared about making decisions or leading a team.'

Hah! Paul didn't need reminding how bossy she'd been. Still was, as far as he could see. Who else would just turn up without an interview invitation? Even so, he'd go through the courtesies of asking her a few questions and then see the other applicants whom he'd actually asked to come here.

'Right,' he said, ten minutes later. 'I'll let you know in a few days.'

Gail gave him a hopeful look. 'That would be great.'

Don't bet on it, he almost said. Instead, he held out his

hand awkwardly. Her hand felt surprisingly soft. 'Good to catch up.'

'It was, wasn't it?' Her eyes were shining. 'I didn't think it would when I first realised it was you. But … well it's been really nice to talk to someone who knew me from my old life, if you know what I mean.'

Yes. And no. There were times when all Paul wanted to do was put his past behind him. Yet Gail was right. There was something about her which made him want to see her again. No. That was ridiculous. The sooner she left, the better.

'See you then.'

Minutes later, Jane put her head round the door. 'The next candidate is ready,' she said. 'Shall I send her in?'

Paul still found it hard sometimes to remember that he was the interviewer and not the interviewee. Aunt Rosemary had given him several pieces of advice but the most important, she'd said, was intuition. You'll know if someone isn't right for the job. Like Gail. But this new applicant, with purple streaks down one side of her hair and tattoos on each bare arm, really wouldn't fit in with the company image. Nor was the next one who kept butting in with questions before he'd finished. The third was clearly more interested in having a good time ('What's the social life here? How many days holiday will I have?'). And another wanted to job-share with her sister so they could both look after each other's children. Paul actually thought this might have been quite a good idea except, as he explained, the role didn't really lend itself to two people doing it. The woman in question then got very irate and threatened to report him to the unions. Was he being unfair? No, Paul told himself. He was a businessman after all. Not a charity worker.

'Looks like you need a cup of tea,' said Jane after the last applicant had left. 'Or something stronger.'

'I'm going to have to re-advertise,' he groaned. 'None of them were any good.'

'Not even the first one who turned up on spec? Gail Lewis? I was quite impressed by her go-for-it attitude. Still …'

Her voice tailed away but Paul understood the meaning behind it all right. 'You're the boss.' That's what she'd meant. 'Even if I don't agree with you.'

Hadn't Paul felt that way about Gail at the airline when she'd made a decision he disapproved of? It made him wonder if he'd been a bit difficult himself.

'By the way, don't forget you asked me to book you dinner at the hotel tonight.'

He often did that, just to check that the service was as it should be for the guests. Maybe tonight's booking was fortuitous.

Paul found his hand punching in the numbers on the phone. Gail's home number from her résumé. Of course she wouldn't be back yet but the answerphone was on.

'Hi. It's me. Paul. Look, there are a few things I'd like to chat about. Not the job. Just … well, other stuff. Are you free by any chance for dinner tonight?'

***

Some hours later, as he was sitting at the Lassiters restaurant table waiting for Gail to turn up, Paul was still no wiser. Why had he invited a woman whom he'd had a 'thing' with and had no intention of rekindling a relationship with? Besides, she had been so bossy at the airline even though, he had to admit, she'd been very efficient. Now she'd be bound to read his invitation as either a 'come on' or the promise of a job which he wasn't going to give her. The only reason he could give for his impulsive suggestion were her eyes. Those sad but also courageous eyes when Gail had been telling him about her marriage break-up. Hadn't he been in that place himself? Of course it was different. In fact, he wouldn't – couldn't – even go there. But it didn't stop him feeling for someone else who was also lonely. And something told him that's exactly what Gail was.

On the other hand, there might be another reason for his so-called 'kind' dinner invitation. Maybe, Paul told himself, he just wanted to gloat. After all, this woman had been a tough cookie. How many times had she reprimanded him for not doing things her way at the airline? Perhaps he subconsciously wanted to rub his good fortune in her face.

No. That wasn't right. Perhaps it was as simple as wanting to have a glamorous escort to show the world that Paul Robinson was quite capable of moving on. Wow. Was that her?

Paul stopped mid-thought as a beautiful brunette in a pale shift dress with matching jacket floated in. Everyone, or so it seemed, stopped to look. Gail looked stunning. She'd put her hair up and was wearing long, sparkly earrings which were classy rather than flashy. She walked with that airline poise which had always made her stand out in a crowd – even amongst the other staff. And she was heading straight for him.

He could feel himself flushing. 'Lovely to see you,' he said. Without meaning to, he brushed her cheek. She smelt good. 'What can I get you to drink?' he said.

'A Chardonnay would be great.'

'I thought we might have champagne, actually.'

'Are we celebrating?'

Why had he said that? 'Look, I need to get something straight, Gail. I didn't think we'd had enough time to catch up before. But – well, there's no easy way of saying this – I don't think it would be a good idea for us to work together.'

Her face sank. 'Really? Because I used to be your boss and also ...'

Her voice tailed off. But there was enough of a suggestion to show that she hadn't forgotten their past either.

'That does have something to do with it.'

She sighed. Then shrugged. 'I did wonder. Never mind. If the worst comes to the worst, I'll probably be able to get a job at my dad's. He owns the garage round the corner from here.'

'Yes, we're on nodding terms,' Paul said uncertainly, recalling Rob Lewis's reputation for being a bit of a hothead. 'It might not be easy to take orders from your dad.'

'He's not that bad, you know. Anyway, you weren't so good at taking orders yourself.'

For a minute, they stared in a hostile fashion at each other. Then they each burst out into peals of laughter. 'Thanks for being honest anyway,' she said. 'And just in case you're wondering, I'm still glad I came. It's amazing here, isn't it?'

'Sure is.' Paul leant towards her across the table. 'See that man to my right? Isn't he that famous actor who ...'

Her eyes widened. 'Yes. It is! Mind you, he's got more hair on screen.'

After that, it was easy to talk. In fact, Paul couldn't remember a time when he'd enjoyed himself so much. Why hadn't it been like this when they'd spent time together in the past? Looking back, he reminded himself that even though he'd initially found Gail attractive back in the airline days, it had been her 'I know best' manner that had made him realise she wasn't the woman for him. But now she seemed like a different person. In fact, her company was distinctly refreshing compared with some of the dates he'd had.

'What's wrong,' asked Gail, seeing his face.

'Nothing.'

'Yes there is. I can tell.'

Paul hadn't intended to talk about Jeremy but there was no getting out of it. 'Well, actually, I was wondering exactly why you and Jeremy broke up. Tell me it's none of my business if you like but you seemed like the perfect couple.'

Gail's eyes immediately lost their sparkle. 'Things aren't always what they seem. If you really want to know, he had one affair too many.'

So he'd been right. 'I'm sorry.'

She reached her hand across the table. 'I'm sorry, too, about your wife.'

'So you heard?'

She nodded. Paul ignored the outstretched hand. Instead, he put his own under the table so he could pierce his hand with his fingernails to ease the pain in his chest.

'Thanks.'

After that, they couldn't quite get back to the conversation they'd had before.

'If you don't mind, I think I'll have an early night,' he said, calling for the waiter to bring the bill.

'Sure.' Gail seemed subdued. 'Thanks for asking me anyway.'

'I'll let you know about the job.'

'Thought you weren't going to give it to me.'

'I'm not but ...'

'Listen, Paul. It's okay. You don't have to say any more. Don't worry about me. I can get a cab home.'

And before he knew it, she was gone.

***

The next day, when Paul was just finishing off a work call in his office, his gran came in. She made a 'Don't worry – I'll wait until you've finished' sign.

Must be urgent. Quickly, Paul ended his call. Not for the first time did he tell himself that having Gran running her chauffeur business 'Home James' from an office next to his was a mixed blessing. In some ways it was great having her near. But in others, it could be tricky. Helen Daniels (as the rest of the world knew her) was a woman to be reckoned with, as was her daughter Rosemary.

'Everything all right?'

'I tried to get hold of you last night, love, but you'd already left the office. I do hope you're going to give the job to that nice girl, Gail. That one had something if you ask me. And she was prepared for emergencies. I bumped into her in the Ladies, you know, and she lent me a pair of tights. Nice quality too.'

Paul gave a short snort. 'Gail always had good taste. But the truth is that she used to be my boss at the airline.' He hesitated, wondering whether to mention they'd had a short relationship. Maybe not. 'And she wasn't easy to be with,' he added.

Helen's neatly-shaped eyebrows rose. 'People with initiative often aren't. Still, it's your call. Must have been nice talking to her anyway. Hear you took her out to dinner.'

'How did you know that?'

'A friend of mine was at Lassiters. Saw your "elegant companion" as she put it. And she was near enough to hear you say her name!'

'Isn't anything private round here?'

'Do I really need to answer that question? By the way, are you doing anything now?'

'No. I'm free actually.'

'Good. Then I'll tell Gail you can see her.'

'What?'

'She's outside in the lobby.'

This was too much! What made Gail think she could just turn up like this? He'd need to put her straight once and for all.

But Gail was chatting to Jane as if they were old friends. She looked stunning, he had to say. That lime green outfit really suited her. Stop. Right there.

'I know what you're going to say,' Gail said, walking towards him. 'I can't keep turning up like this without an appointment. And you're right. I don't want you to think I'm being bossy or anything like that …'

'Heaven forbid,' muttered Paul.

'… but I just felt we left the evening on a bit of a

downer. Can I take you out to lunch? I can't stretch to anywhere smart like last night but I spotted a nice coffee shop opposite.'

'Why?'

Paul didn't mean to sound rude but it was too late.

'Why?' repeated Gail. 'It will give us a chance to carry on catching up. You know, I got the feeling last night that we might have more in common than we'd thought. Just as friends, of course.'

'Of course.' He knew what she meant. It was surprisingly easy to talk to her.

This became even more obvious over lunch. Gail opened up quite a bit about her heartbreak with Jeremy, telling him how her ex was now bombarding her with postcards and letters asking to meet up again.

'You're not going to forgive him, are you?' he said.

'No way.'

Paul didn't know why he felt relieved. But he did.

'I really meant it when I said I was sorry about your Terry,' said Gail quietly. 'I knew someone once who committed suicide. It was an old school friend. She ...'

'Please. Don't. I can't talk about it.'

'I'm the one who should be sorry ...'

'No. It's me. It's just that ...'

'You don't have to say any more. Me and my big mouth.'

'Gail! There you are!'

'Dad?'

A big man in greasy blue overalls and a baseball cap strode right over and plonked himself down at the table as if he'd been invited.

'I've just been into your office to ask your gran if our

Gail got the job.'

Gail looked as though she wished the floor would open up and swallow her. 'Why didn't you ask me instead?'

'Because someone was out last night, weren't they? And by the time you got back, I was asleep. Then when I woke in the morning, you'd already gone. Anyway, I needed to talk to Helen about Neighbourhood Watch. Well, actually, I didn't but I thought it would be an excuse. When Helen said you'd been into the offices, I asked if you'd got the job ...'

'Oh Dad, you didn't.'

'Well, turns out I was right! Otherwise why would you have had dinner last night – Helen told me that one – and now lunch? I asked her if that's how her grandson conducts all his interviews! So tell me. Did you get it?'

'We're just catching up, Dad. And for your information, Paul isn't going to give me the job.'

'Just because you were his boss before? Thought you were more of a man than that.' He glowered at Paul. 'Your loss, mate. My Gail would be brilliant in that job of yours. No one has as much initiative as she has.'

Paul stood up.

'I'm afraid I'm going to have to go now. I've got a meeting. Nice to see you, Rob.'

That was awkward. The man was acting as if his daughter was a kid who needed her hand held! Behind him he could hear Gail saying 'Now look what you've done, Dad. You've completely ruined any chance I might still have had.'

**

That night Paul couldn't sleep. His dreams were haunted by Terry and also Gail. 'Give me a chance,' one of them was crying. He just didn't know which.

'There's someone to see you in your office,' said Jane when he arrived.

No guesses as to who that might be.

'Gail. Fancy seeing you here. Again.'

'I'm sorry. I know I shouldn't keep doing this. But I had to apologise for Dad. He really shouldn't have ...'

'No. He was right.'

She looked confused. 'What do you mean?'

'Anyone with as much determination as you deserves the job. Your dad isn't the only one who thinks that. So do my gran and PA. And because I value their opinions, I'm finally coming round to their point of view. You're hired.'

'Really?'

'Really. On one condition.'

'What's that?'

He faced her squarely so there could be no doubt. 'Just remember who's the boss.'

Three

GAIL

How she loved her new job! Sometimes Gail had to pinch herself. There wasn't a minute to get bored or – more importantly – to think about Jeremy. She'd put his last postcard straight in the bin without even looking at it.

Paul was a different person to work with here than at the airline. Of course, it made a difference that he was the boss this time and not her. But she had to admit that he had some good ideas.

For a start, the hotel was thinking of buying a minibus, so they could pick up guests from the airport. When she mentioned that to her dad over tea one night, he got really excited.

'They'll need a mechanic to service it, won't they? Someone who they can rely on. Someone they already know.'

'Are you fishing for business, Dad?' asked Gail, looking disapprovingly at the number of potatoes on her father's plate. Since moving in with him, she'd tried to get him to eat more sensibly. She worried that ever since Mum's death, Dad hadn't been looking after himself very well, and he was definitely drinking too much.

'What's wrong with that? We all know each other, don't we? Like I said, it's better than Paul doing a deal with an outsider. And before you answer, don't try putting any more of that salad on my plate.'

No flies on him! Gail shook her head in mock indignation.

'You need to eat more healthily and cut down on the booze. And – well, don't take this the wrong way – you've also got to realise that we might be living under the same roof but you can't use me to do you any favours.'

'You work for the man, don't you? What's wrong with putting a good word in for me?'

'Because it wouldn't be professional. If you want to put yourself up for this, great. But it's between you and Paul. I suggest you make an appointment with him.'

Rob made a disappointed face and then wiped his mouth on his sleeve. 'Always were stubborn, weren't you?'

'I just wanted to get everything straight. And while we're on this subject, I'd like to make it clear that my situation here is only temporary. Don't get me wrong. I'm grateful to you for putting me up but this place is too small for both of us. Nice as it is to be together, I'm going to have to get my life back on track soon and strike out on my own.'

He nodded. 'I know, my girl. It's not easy for you.'

Gail felt a lump in her throat. It wasn't easy for him

either after Mum.

Meanwhile, she had enough on her plate with her new role. It was important to make her mark with some suggestions of her own but at the same time, she didn't want to tread on anyone's toes. In a way, it wasn't that dissimilar from the airline where you had to keep everyone happy. That included making sure that she got Paul's approval for new projects.

**

It wasn't easy sharing an office with the boss. In fact, she'd been really surprised when Paul had explained there wasn't another room available for her. So the following day, when she went in, Gail got a real shock.

'Paul! I wonder if I could just ask you …' Then she stopped, taking in the other man who was there too. 'Dad? I'm sorry. I didn't realise you two were having a meeting.'

'Thought I'd ask your boss if he'd like me to do the car servicing for Lassiters.'

So that's why he was wearing a suit instead of his usual blue overalls and baseball cap!

'I gather you told your father about the minibus scheme,' said Paul, looking straight at her.

'Well, yes, but I said he'd need to talk to you. It's nothing to do with me.'

'Right. Well, Rob, I'll definitely bear you in mind then.'

Paul rose to his feet, clearly indicating the interview was over.

'You're not going to make a decision now then?'

'Dad,' whispered Gail warningly. Couldn't he see he was pushing it a bit?

'Well, to be honest, I'm interested. But I'll need a couple of days to think about it. So like I said, I'll let you know.'

'Sure.' Rob winked at her. 'Don't let the boss keep you too late tonight, love. I'm cooking tea.'

Gail groaned as the door closed behind him. 'I'm really sorry,' she said to Paul. 'I only mentioned the minibus in passing. When he said he wanted to get involved, I told him to talk to you. I don't want you thinking that ...'

'That he's got an advantage because I'm employing his daughter?' To her relief, Paul's eyes were twinkling. 'No, of course I don't.' He glanced at the papers in her hands. 'Looks like you wanted to talk to me about something. I've got ten minutes before my next meeting. Will that be enough?'

'Sure.'

Quickly Gail launched into her plan to encourage more business to the hotel by offering special rates for returning clients.

'Great idea! I knew you were the right person for promotions manager.'

'Thanks.' Gail flushed with pleasure. He was taking her seriously! Jeremy had never done this when it came to work. As far as her ex had been concerned, her airline job was just an excuse to see the world. Gail's estimation of Paul was going up.

But her dad's surprise arrival at the office niggled all day. He needed to remember that this was her job and her reputation. She couldn't be seen to be acting in a biased manner.

She told him as much that night over tea.

'Don't get so uptight about it,' he said. 'Anyway, Jim

Robinson reckons I might be in with a chance.'

'What? You've spoken to Paul's father?'

'Don't look like that. We just had a beer at The Waterhole. Happened to bump into him on my way out.'

'Did you ask him to push your case?'

Rob had the grace to look slightly bashful. 'In a way.'

'And what did he say?'

Rob helped himself to seconds. 'That Paul doesn't like anyone interfering in his business dealings.'

'Exactly!'

'But I've got another idea too.'

Rob went on to explain that the Robinsons' neighbour in Ramsay Street, Harold Bishop, had money to invest. Okay, so he was as an old stick-in-the-mud, but investment was exactly what Rob needed if he was to grow the business.

Gail had to admit that it made sense.

'Tell you what,' said Rob with a grin, 'if I have a few more of those salad leaves and skip a third lot of potatoes, will you stop looking so serious? I hope you're going out tonight to have some fun.'

Gail got up to clear the dishes. 'Actually I was thinking of an early night.'

'So you're not seeing Jeremy then?'

Gail stopped in her tracks. 'What do you mean?'

Rob pointed to the answerphone which, Gail could see now, was flashing. 'Just that he's left you two messages, asking you to call him.'

Dumping down the plates, she marched straight across and pressed the Delete button.

'You're not even going to play them back?'

'No. Anyway, there's no need if you've already

listened to them.'

Rob nodded. 'I'm glad you said that. He never made you happy. No. Don't deny it. I know my daughter better than she realises. Now Paul on the other hand ...'

'Paul and I are just good friends.'

'Is that so? Glad to hear it. Because I seem to remember that when you worked together at the airline, you got close for a time. Then you decided that he was a pain in the ...'

'Well, things have changed. Now, if you don't mind, Dad, I'm going for a walk to clear my head. Maybe you'd like to do the dishes instead.'

'Say no more, love. Say no more.'

***

A couple of days later, Gail was drawing up a new spreadsheet when Paul came up to her desk. 'Got a second?'

Before she could say yes, he'd sat on the edge of her desk. Was this an informal chat then? She felt a bit awkward but at the same time, surprisingly flattered.

'Guess where I've been?'

Gail hated guessing games. After Jeremy, all she wanted was a straightforward life. No more games. Both in her private and working life.

'I don't know.'

'It's all right. Don't look so worried. I've been round to your dad's garage to sign the contracts.'

Gail couldn't help clapping her hands together. 'That's great!'

Paul looked pleased too. 'I told him that as long as he can cope with all the work involved then we have a deal.

Your dad was pretty chuffed. Couldn't get me round there fast enough to do the paperwork. I've given him a good deal too, if you ask me. But that's because I know I'm getting one too. He works hard, he's got the skills and I know him.'

Gail flushed with pleasure. 'Thanks, Paul. I know he won't let you down.'

'Look, how about you and I go out to lunch tomorrow to celebrate?'

'Shouldn't that be you two instead of me?'

'I thought we could use the opportunity to go over some work things too.' He got up from the desk. 'I know it's a Saturday. Maybe you've got something planned …'

'Can I think about it?'

'Sure. Just give me a ring.'

What was wrong with her, Gail asked herself. It was only a working lunch. Wasn't it?

'Just be careful love,' said her father when she found herself telling him that evening. 'You've been hurt once before.'

'It's not like that with Paul and me.'

'I'm not saying it is. I just don't want to see you upset again. And for what it's worth, I'm glad you deleted Jeremy's messages.' He gave Gail a brief cuddle. 'I'm proud of you for being strong.'

***

Paul took Gail to a restaurant on the outskirts of town. 'Thought we'd go somewhere that wasn't anything to do with the Corporation,' he said. 'You know, I'm really pleased with the way things are working out. I did the right thing in hiring you, Gail. Even though I know we both had our doubts.'

'We certainly did!'

'You mean you almost turned me down?'

'I might have but ...'

'But what?'

His eyes held hers for a second longer than necessary.

'It just seemed the right thing to do,' she said.

'I know what you mean. Now, how about we order? I think I'm going for the prawns.'

Gail began to giggle.

'What's so funny?'

'Remember that time at the airline when one of the girls dropped a prawn down the front of that passenger with the low top?'

Paul burst out into laughter. 'I do. And what about that day when ...'

Afterwards, Gail returned home feeling as though the time had whizzed by. She spent the Sunday having a good tidy up round the unit (how she missed having a place of her own) and was at her desk early on Monday morning. That was odd. She could hear Dad's voice in the corridor outside.

'I didn't realise you wanted me to do car cleaning and detailing too.'

'It was in the contract.'

'I'm not sure I can handle all of that too.'

'Then I might have to look elsewhere.'

Gail gave a silent gasp. Clearly her dad hadn't read the small print properly. Now he was going to go and lose the deal.

'Okay. I'll make it happen.'

'Sure?'

'Yes. I was just a bit taken aback that's all. By the way, I heard you had a nice lunch with my girl on Saturday.'

'We did.'

Paul's tone was guarded.

'Don't look so embarrassed! You know, I told her to watch out for you ...'

'You did?'

'And for all the other blokes who are sniffing round after her. You can't blame me. I'm her dad. You know I used to think you were a bit full of yourself. But you're not so bad as I thought.'

How awful! Gail wanted to sink into the ground. Should she say anything to Paul? No. Best to pretend she hadn't heard anything. She only hoped the others hadn't either.

***

By the following week, when her dad brought the first serviced car back to the hotel, Gail was worried about something else. 'I think you're doing too much,' she told him quietly. 'You need someone to help you.'

'Okay, okay. Got time for a coffee? It is nearly lunchtime, isn't it. There's something I want to talk over.'

'What is it?'

'Wait till we're sitting down. Latte, is it?'

Gail was beginning to feel nervous.

'The thing is, love, that I'm changing my mind about your Paul.'

'He isn't *my* Paul! He's my boss.'

'Whatever. He'd be a good catch. I'm telling you that.'

'Dad. Like I said. He's my boss and we're just good friends.'

'Yeah, yeah. But a woman is entitled to change her mind. Isn't she?'

Four

PAUL

'Paul? I'm glad I've got you. There's something important I need to discuss.'

It was Aunt Rosemary from the States. No asking how he was or apologies for ringing at 6 a.m. Instead, she was straight down to business as usual.

'You'll be receiving a visit soon from a very important Japanese contact, Toshiro Udagawa. He's thinking of doing some business with us and I can't emphasise enough how vital this is to the corporation. It's essential, Paul, that you do anything it takes to make sure that this deal goes through. And I mean anything.'

This sounded serious. Toshiro Udagawa already had several successful business interests in Erinsborough. 'I'll do what I can.'

'No, Paul. You won't just do what you can. You'll pull it off. Okay? One word of warning. Toshiro has extremely strong family values so it might be best not to mention …'

There was a brief pause but Paul knew exactly what his aunt was going to say. 'I don't want to mention my past any more than you do,' he said quickly.

'Thank you. I hope you don't mind me mentioning it.'

As if I don't think of it every day myself, thought Paul. Terry's final moments still haunted him. What other husband would refuse to see his wife after she'd begged him to forgive her? If he had, she might still be alive.

'I also wanted to know how Gail was doing,' continued Aunt Rosemary.

Paul was relieved to change subjects. 'Very well. I'm impressed. She's got some good ideas and she's extremely professional. Everyone likes her.'

'Good. Make sure she's part of the welcoming committee for Toshiro then. Must dash now. Good to talk.'

Paul put down the receiver feeling decidedly unsettled. It wasn't the prospect of reeling in a new client that troubled him. This was exactly the kind of challenge he liked. No, it was the memories which his aunt had brought up. Suicide left an indelible 'guilty' mark on those who were left behind. You never stopped wondering if there was something you could have done to prevent it.

Had Terry realised that when she'd killed herself? Was this her final act of revenge? Or was it the act of a desperate woman behind bars?

***

GAIL

How fast the weeks were going. Easter was almost here. Everyone in the office was giving each other little baskets. Gail wasn't going to bother but Paul had been so good to her dad that on impulse, she bought him an egg.

'That's really nice of you.' Paul looked genuinely thrilled. 'No one's got me one of those for … well, for years. I'm sorry but I didn't get you one. But I have got you this …'

A bonus!

'Wow. Thanks. I wasn't expecting one. I mean, not so fast.'

'That's because you're proving your worth.'

He glanced at the clock. It was nearly one o'clock.

'Can I get you some lunch? I'm just going out to get some myself,' Gail offered.

'I'd love to – I'm really hungry – but I've got to get everything sorted for Mr Udagawa.'

'I've heard the name around the office but I don't know any more.'

Paul looked worried and excited at the same time. He explained the set up to Gail. Toshiro Udagawa was a Japanese businessman planning to build a manufacturing plant in Australia. It would be a joint venture with the Daniels Corporation.

'Mmm. Sounds like an important deal for us.'

'It is, and it would create local jobs too.'

'You're always thinking of others, Paul.' She gave a wry smile.

They were back to their usual bantering but unlike

their time at the airline there was genuine friendship there too.

'Well,' she added, 'I'll leave you to it. But I'll bring back some lunch. It's such a lovely day. Shame we can't have it outside instead of in the office.'

'Tell you what. If I can get through this paperwork while you've gone, we might just do that.'

***

How lovely it was to sit by the water. It was really easy to talk to Paul. Gail even found herself telling Paul about her dad's change of heart. 'I know you two haven't exactly seen eye to eye in the past but he really likes you now.'

Then she blushed, remembering her father's conversation with Paul in the office.

'I'm just pleased that we can be friends without romance getting in the way.'

'Exactly!'

Phew! So he felt the same as her.

'Being friends is far less complicated.'

Briefly, he put a hand on hers. 'I couldn't agree more. By the way, Gran wondered if you'd like to come round for dinner next week. Would Tuesday work for you?'

'Great! I'll look forward to it.'

Five

GAIL

Gail felt a buzz of excitement as she got ready for dinner with the Robinsons. In a close-knit suburb like Erinsborough, they were well known, Dad had told her, especially in Ramsay Street where everyone soon got to know each other's business. But when you'd been away like she had, things changed. So Dad had filled her in on the bits she didn't know.

Paul's wife Terry had died. Suicide, Dad had said. How awful. Poor man. How did you even start to deal with something like that? Maybe that's why he was always in the office. Distraction, as she'd learned, was the best way to deal with the obstacles which fate sometimes hurled at you.

Meanwhile, she needed to get a move on. Now what should she wear? Helen was always so elegant. Gail needed to make sure she matched up to the occasion. Maybe this simple dress in duck egg blue would do.

Gail's heart started to beat rather nervously as she walked up to the door of Number 26. It wasn't every day you went for dinner with your new boss's family!

'Come on in, Gail!' Helen was standing at the door before she'd even had a chance to knock. She was wearing a chic but casual green and black print blouse and, once more, Gail was struck by the older woman's style as well as what appeared to be genuine warmth. 'How lovely you look. I'm so glad you could come.'

'Thank you for asking me,' replied Gail, looking around. This was so much bigger and brighter than Dad's unit.

'Paul, dear, our guest has arrived.'

'Hi!' Her boss seemed less confident than in the office. Maybe he was regretting mixing business with pleasure. 'Can I take your jacket?'

His arm brushed hers awkwardly as he led her into a lovely airy room with modern, stylish furniture.

'I like your home.'

Paul shook his head. 'Well, it's the family home, but I see it as Gran and Dad's place now that I live at the hotel.'

'Don't get me onto that!' Helen was rolling her eyes as if dealing with a naughty child. 'I wanted him to move in with us but he chose to stay at Lassiters.'

'That's because he's a grown man, Helen. He's used to his independence.'

Jim Robinson!

'Great to see you, Gail. Make yourself at home.'

Nervously, she sat on the edge of the sofa, eyeing this tall good-looking man with distinguished grey hair. He had a certain similarity to his son – without the grey, of course! Back in the airline days all the girls had fancied Paul. She'd felt quite flattered when he asked her out but it was pretty clear by the third date that they weren't going to work out. He was so bossy! Still, Paul seemed to have changed now. He'd been surprisingly kind when she'd told him about her divorce. And he was still attractive. Not, of course, that she was interested. Meanwhile, his father was making her nervous as if he could read her thoughts!

'It's good of you to ask me round,' she said.

'Nonsense!' Jim pressed a cool glass of white wine into her hand. 'The more the merrier! Helen loves to pack the house with friends and family, don't you?'

The older woman gave a little sigh. 'It feels very quiet at times compared with the old days.' Then she sat down next to Gail. 'I'm not sure if you know our story, Gail, but Jim and I brought up the kids together after my daughter died.'

'Paul told me. I'm sorry.'

Helen gave the sort of gesture people make when something hurts but they don't want to show it. 'I have to say that even though it was pretty hectic, I really miss everyone being at home. Mind you, we still have Lucy and Scott, thank goodness.'

'Not for much longer,' added Paul, with a twinkle in his eye. He seemed to be thawing a bit now, observed Gail. 'My little brother and Charlene are getting pretty serious.'

Gail was beginning to feel a bit muddled. 'Charlene?'

'Poor you! We're throwing all these names at you as if you ought to know them. Charlene lives in the street. You'll meet her when they come over in a minute.'

Gail felt her stomach wobble with nerves at the thought of being introduced to more people. It was odd. In her old job she'd loved dealing with strangers. But the divorce and the change in her life had taken away some of that confidence. Now she was finally getting back on her feet, thanks to the job with Paul, and it felt important to make a good impression.

'I know you'll get on really well,' continued Helen. 'Charlene's a lively girl. She and Scott make a perfect couple.'

Paul got up abruptly. 'You're such a romantic, Gran.'

'There's a lot to be said for it, darling. Look at Julie!'

Another name!

'She's my older sister,' explained Paul, seeing her confusion. 'Julie's married but she lives out of state. You could say that she's the one who got away! Only joking, Gran!'

Gail took a sip of wine while trying to get the family tree straight in her head. 'And Lucy is your little sister, right?' she added.

Paul's eyes softened. 'She's a cute kid. Right now, she's in Europe on a trip. I just hope she's behaving herself.'

Helen threw him an affectionate glance. 'Dear Paul. He's the protective big brother!'

How nice! Not for the first time, Gail wondered what it would be like to be part of a big family. How lovely it would be to have all that support and love.

'What about you?' asked Paul, topping up her glass.

Gail was usually very careful about how much she drank but tonight she was feeling rather out of her depth. Maybe it was being on her own for so long but she wasn't used to so many people around her in a social situation. 'It's just me and Dad,' she said, trying to sound light. 'Sadly, we lost Mum a while back.'

'You don't have any brothers or sisters then?'

It struck her as he spoke that through all that time at the airline, they'd rarely discussed their private lives.

'No. It must be great to have each other.'

'Hah! Sometimes. And sometimes not.'

Jim butted in. 'My son doesn't mean that. In fact, it looks like you're going to meet Scott and Charlene now. I can hear them at the door.'

'Hi everyone!'

Helen was right! The pretty young woman with long, curly hair that came bouncing in was obviously madly in love with the handsome Scott. Now she thought of it, Gail had seen them walking around the Lassiters Complex, hand in hand. She just hadn't realised they were part of Paul's family.

'You must be Gail,' said the young man, shaking her hand politely. 'I've heard a lot about you.'

'Really?' Gail felt herself flushing.

'We thought it was nice that you'd moved in with your dad,' said Paul quickly.

'I was worried about him. Since Mum went, he's been steadily going downhill and not looking after himself properly.' Oh dear, she hadn't meant to say so much but the Robinsons' confidences had made her open up.

'Heard you've had your own troubles too.' This was Jim. 'Still, it's good that the two of you have each other. Families need to stick together in times of trouble.'

Clearly they were talking about her divorce from Jeremy. Gail felt a prickle of resentment. If they expected her to bare her heart, they were wrong. She'd come here to make a new start and get on with life.

Luckily Helen seemed to sense her discomfort. 'You two have arrived just in time for dinner,' she said, giving Charlene and Scott a hug. 'Now how about the pair of you show Gail the way?'

The table was beautifully laid with pink napkins and candles in the middle.

'Wow!' breathed Charlene. 'Is it someone's birthday?'

Helen looked pleased. 'I just wanted to make a special effort to welcome the latest addition to the Daniels Corporation.'

Gail felt embarrassed but also touched. 'That's very kind of you.'

Jim lifted his glass. 'How about a toast? To Gail!'

'Don't give her too much to drink,' said Paul who was sitting opposite, 'or she won't be able to do enough work tomorrow.' Then he winked to indicate it was just a joke.

As the meal progressed, Gail began to relax more. Scott and Charlene were, she noticed, holding hands under the table. So sweet! How she could remember being in love at that age …

'So tell me, Gail,' said Scott leaning across towards her. 'What was it like working with my big brother at the airline? Was he as tough then as he is now?'

'Actually, I was his boss.'

'No!' Scott slapped his thigh with excitement. 'You didn't tell us that, Paul!'

'Yes, well, that was a long time ago.'

Gail almost felt sorry for him. He looked so embarrassed. 'Actually, we made a good team.' Oh dear, she could feel herself flushing. 'I mean we all did.' She shot a 'help-me' look at Paul.

'We did indeed,' he said firmly. 'A better airline crew you'd never find.'

'Is that right?' asked Scott his eyes twinkling. He knows, thought Gail. He can sense that there was something between Paul and me. Better change the subject fast.

'What delicious fish,' she said.

'Thank you.' Helen seemed pleased by the compliment. 'I bought it this morning from ... oh dear. Is that the phone? Why do people ring at mealtimes? Excuse me a moment. And you two!' She looked meaningfully in Scott and Charlene's direction. 'Don't think you can use my absence as an excuse to kiss at the table!'

Gail couldn't help joining in the giggles.

'So,' asked Jim, directly. 'How are you settling in to Erinsborough?'

'Pretty well, thanks.' Gail glanced at Paul briefly. 'I'm enjoying my job.'

'Great. My son tells me you've got some good ideas.'

Paul gave her an encouraging smile. 'We're glad to have you.'

'But it must be different, love.' Jim looked more serious. 'I know you used to work at the same airline as my son, and then, of course, you got married to that famous racing driver. Jeremy, isn't it?'

'Dad,' began Paul.

Thank goodness Helen came back in at that point. 'It was Rosemary,' she said, sitting down again. 'I explained we were eating so we're going to talk later.'

Gail seized on the chance to change the subject from her ex. 'Rosemary's your daughter, isn't she?'

Helen nodded. 'My other one.'

Instantly Gail felt terrible. Of course. Helen's other daughter was the one who had died when giving birth to little Lucy. Even when someone was dead, they still counted as someone's child or spouse or parent.

'Rosemary's the big chief in the family,' said Jim. 'When she says jump, we all do.'

'Now, now.' Helen looked displeased. 'Your sister-in-law is a businesswoman. You don't get to where she is in life by not giving orders, as my eldest grandson knows.'

Gail glanced across at her boss, who was making a rueful expression. 'It's why I need your help, Gail. We run a tight ship.'

'And I'm happy to be on board.'

'Wonderful!' Helen clapped her hands together. 'Now how about dessert? I've got peach mousse and home-made ice cream. Afterwards, I thought we'd take a look through some family photographs. Then Gail will be able to know exactly who she's dealing with!'

***

Helen was as good as her word. No sooner had she helped to clear the plates ('Please, Helen, I'd like to help') than Gail found herself surrounded by albums back in the lounge room. Scott and Charlene had shot off by then, making their apologies and putting their arms around each other as they left.

'Gran!' groaned Paul. 'Do we have to go through this?'

'Absolutely! This one was taken when Paul was only six. Isn't he cute in those short trousers?'

Paul pretended to cover his eyes.

'And here he is at ten, after winning the school running race. I've got the trophy somewhere …'

'Honestly, Gran. Enough is enough! As for you, Gail, I'm going to bribe your dad into showing me the Lewis family album one day.'

'No way!'

That reminded her. 'Do you know anything about Harold investing in Dad's garage?' asked Gail as Paul showed her to her car later that evening.

'Actually my dad said something about him and Harold going over to your place to talk about it. The three of them are thinking about a partnership.'

'That's good. I haven't seen Dad so excited about something for years – not since he worked on racing cars. Your deal has given him a real boost too. I'm so happy for him.'

Paul took her hand. 'That's what I like about you, Gail. You're caring. I'm just sorry that you've been hurt.'

'And I'm sorry life's been tough for you too,' she said softly.

He stepped back.

Instantly Gail realised she should never have mentioned Terry, even though she hadn't actually said her name.

'Well, it's nice to have seen you,' he now said stiffly. 'I'm going to be pretty busy in the next few days with Mr Udagawa's visit. So I might not see you for a bit.'

'I understand. Good luck.'

'Thanks.'

Well done, Gail told herself as she drove back. She'd gone and messed up what had been a really nice evening. Clearly Paul was still hurt by the past, no matter how hard he put a brave face on it. After all, it took one damaged survivor to recognise another.

Six

PAUL

'Hi! Are you free by any chance?' asked Gail.

At first it had been quite strange sharing his office with someone else but now Paul was beginning to like it – especially as Gail was always so bouncy and chatty. It reminded him of the attractive girl he'd known at the airline before he'd realised that she could be so bossy. Then again, that had been a long time ago. They'd both changed.

'Sure.' He waved to the chair opposite the desk but somehow that seemed too formal. 'Actually, let's take a seat over here, shall we?' That was better. There was a great view out of the window and it was more casual.

Gail perched on her seat. She was wearing, he noticed, a skirt that suited her figure, and a white blouse. The same colour that Terry had been wearing when he'd last seen her ...

'Anything wrong?'

Quickly Paul pulled himself together. 'No. Just a bit tired, that's all.'

'We can do this another time.'

'It's fine. Tell me what you want.'

Oh dear. Now he was sounding too abrupt.

Gail handed him a sheet of notes. 'I just wanted to run these ideas past you. I think we could do with running an ad campaign to promote the restaurant.'

'I've been wondering about that too.' Great minds think alike, he almost said. 'I'll come back to you when I've had a chance to go through it. Meanwhile, I wanted to talk to you about Udagawa. His plane will be touching down very soon.'

'The Japanese businessman?'

'That's right. I've arranged for him to be met at the airport but wondered if you could show him around. You know, be a sort of hostess.'

'Hostess?'

She raised her eyes.

'Not like that. Only in a platonic sense.' Paul could feel himself going bright red.

'Only joking. I know what you meant but you have to be careful with the hostess word! It can mean all kinds of different things.' She crossed her legs. Was that intentional? No. Gail wasn't like that. At least he didn't think so.

'Love to,' she said brightly. 'I'll draw up an itinerary. When do I start?'

Paul glanced at his watch. 'Could you be at the hotel when he arrives in just over an hour? I know that doesn't give you much notice but ...'

'No problem.' She jumped to her feet. 'Remember

what we used to say at the airline? Anything's possible. The sky's the limit.'

How could he have forgotten?

'Talking of possibilities,' he said, 'I gather from my dad that things are really progressing at the garage. This three man partnership is almost finalised – apparently Harold just wants his solicitor to go over the fine print.'

'I hope it's going to work out between the three of them.'

'Me too.'

'You know,' she continued as they headed for the door, 'I don't want you to think that I had anything to do with this. My work and our dads' deal, well, it's separate. I'd just like to make that clear.'

'Don't worry. I know that. You just concentrate on Mr Udagawa. He could be really important to the business.'

'It's okay. I won't let you down.'

'I didn't mean that,' Paul tried to say. Too late. She'd already gone.

Paul spent the next couple of hours going through the pile of papers on his desk – including Gail's ideas. They were good! He'd made the right decision there even if he hadn't been sure at first. Maybe he had Gran to thank for that. But what Gail said just now was true. They couldn't allow family to get in the way of business. And Gail's dad seemed to think there was more going on between his daughter and Paul than there really was.

He was so engrossed in his thoughts that he almost didn't hear the phone going.

'Paul?'

'Dad ...'

'You're not going to believe this, son. Rob and I went

round to Number 32 so Harold can read through the contract again. I thought it was more or less sorted but you know Harold. Always fussy.'

Or maybe just careful?

'And then Harold wanted to look round the garage, and said the workshop was "too dirty" and he won't commit any money until he's sure everything is as it should be. You can imagine how that went down with Gail's dad. Kept going on about how the place wasn't meant to be a beauty salon.'

Paul was beginning to sense real trouble brewing.

'I told Rob not to say anything that will upset Harold until after he's signed on the dotted line, then we can handle him.'

'That might not be so easy, Dad. But you're right. Just get the contracts signed before Harold changes his mind. Look, I'm really sorry but I've got to go now. I've got this really important businessman turning up ...'

'The Japanese one?'

'That's right. Gail's going to be showing him around.'

'Well, you can't go wrong there. Just wish her father had her tact. Your gran thinks she's great.'

'Yes. Well, like I say, I'm going to have to go. See you later at the house? Okay.'

As if he didn't have enough on his plate without having to handle his father's business worries too.

***

'Mr Udagawa! Welcome to the Daniels Corporation. I trust you had a good flight.'

Their guest nodded. He wore a well-cut grey business suit and steel glasses as if he was used to poring over facts and figures. For some reason he was a bit older than Paul had imagined – more like Dad's age than his own.

'Very good, thank you. And it was extremely pleasant to be received by such a delightful hostess when I arrive at hotel.'

Paul caught Gail's eye.

'Thank you,' she said. 'We just want to make sure that you have a very pleasant stay.'

'Is someone going to introduce me?'

It was Helen, coming into the office from her own, and wearing a very fetching yellow suit. The colour really suited her silver hair.

'Mr Udagawa, this is my grandmother, Mrs Daniels.'

'Helen. Please.'

The businessman bowed. 'Very good to meet you.'

'I believe that Gail is going to be showing you around.'

'Indeed but I am rather tired now. I have, what do you call it, jet lag. So I will rest until after dinner. Then your Miss Gail has arranged an evening out for all of us.'

'We're looking forward to it.'

The evening was a great success even though it was dominated by Mr Udagawa showing them photographs of his family.

'What a charming man,' said Helen, when their guest went to the bathroom. 'I always like someone with family values.'

Gail went red. Maybe she was thinking of her own marriage.

Paul felt he needed to reassure her. 'I reckon we're impressing him pretty well,' he said quickly.

With any luck, they'd get this deal in the bag. They

certainly needed it. If only to prove to Rosemary that he was up to the job.

***

The next few days were pretty hectic. Paul did his best to free up office time to help Gail entertain Mr Udagawa but it was full-on. And there were still no certainties that he was going to give them his custom. The good thing was that Dad, Rob and Harold had finally signed the contracts for the garage. 'Seems like Harold isn't going to be the silent partner we thought he might be. He's setting up an office in the garage!'

Clearly this was worrying Gail too. 'My dad's furious at what he sees as interference,' she said during a quick debriefing session in between entertaining their Japanese guest. 'I had to remind him that he might have started the business, but he could have gone under if it hadn't been for Jim and Harold. Every partnership relies on compromise and he's just going to have to get used to it.'

Paul couldn't help feeling this was slightly ironic. Hadn't Gail had to get used to being his employee rather than his boss? In fact, he admired the way she'd done it. 'You're right. But let's get down to our own business, shall we? I've just been talking to Rosemary on the phone. She's pleased with how it's all going with Mr U.'

'He's certainly keeping me busy. How many more photographs am I going to have to sit through?'

'And this picture is of my wife's second cousin once removed,' joked Paul in a mock accent. Then he stopped himself. 'Actually, I feel a bit envious. I like their sense of values in Japan, and the way Udagawa treats his staff like family.'

'Talking of family,' said Gail, lightly touching him on the arm. 'Mr U did keep asking me about your own marital prospects. Just thought I ought to warn you in case he brings up the subject. I mean he knows you're a widower but … I wouldn't like it to get awkward for you.'

That was nice. Instinctively, Paul reached across with his arm to pull her closer to him. Instantly he realised from her face that he'd made a mistake. He drew back. 'Time to get back to work, I think.'

***

If they hadn't already arranged to have dinner at Lassiters restaurant the next day Paul might have cancelled it after that. He should never have been so demonstrative but hopefully Gail would just see it as a friendly gesture. And that's all it was. Right?

Anyway, it was a business dinner to catch up on everything. Not just Mr U's visit but also general matters.

Paul had dressed carefully. Not too formal but smart enough to complement Gail. She looked lovely as she always did. If anything, she looked more lovely than when she'd worked at the airline. Maybe that's because she was less pushy now. Or had that just been the old him, misreading her?

'So what do you think?' Gail was looking at him, clearly expecting a reply. 'Do you agree that we should send Jane on a business admin course to improve her skills and keep her loyal to the company?'

'Great idea. I admire your business skills.'

She blushed, toying with her chocolate mousse. 'And I admire yours too. Now about yesterday …'

'I'm sorry.'

'What for?'

'I didn't mean to ...'

He stopped as she blushed again.

'I'm not sure what you're referring to, Paul, but I'm talking about Mr U. He keeps going on about whether you have plans to marry again. It's really rather embarrassing. So you might need a good answer up your sleeve. I've got a feeling that your attitude to family values could make or break this deal.'

'It's really none of his business, but I see your point.' To cover his confusion, Paul called over the waiter, even though they'd only just finished their meal. 'Can we have the bill? Thanks.'

'Hello, Gail!'

They both looked up. Paul's heart sank. He'd seen Jeremy a couple of times when Gail had been working at the airline and, of course, many times in the papers. But Gail's ex appeared even more suave and handsome than ever. Then again, why should that bother him?

'Jeremy?'

Gail's face was shocked. Upset. Angry. Some of the other diners had noticed her raised voice and were now staring.

'I've been eating here myself – I'm staying at the hotel, and just happened to notice you. Rather lucky, don't you think? We've got a lot of catching up to do.'

'And what makes you think that?' Gail stood up. 'Look, You're interrupting a business meeting. I don't know what you're playing at but just leave me alone. Got it?'

Seven

GAIL

Gail couldn't sleep a wink that night. Her head was buzzing. How dare Jeremy come up to her like that in the restaurant? Was it really a coincidence that he'd seen her? Or was he stalking her? After all, he'd been sending her enough postcards in the last few weeks.

It wasn't fair. Hadn't he hurt her enough already without trying to interfere in her new life? Talking of which, it was already time to leave for the office. How was she going to do a full day's work on so little sleep?

'Come on,' she told herself in the mirror, slapping on some concealer under her eyes. 'You can do this.'

But inside, she felt really uneasy. As though something was going to happen. Something she had no control over …

Paul was already in their office when she arrived. Gail kept her head down, barely raising her head to say hello.

'Everything all right?'

'Fine,' she said crisply. 'I'm just trying to finish this report, that's all.'

'That's not what I meant.' He was coming closer. For a minute, she thought he was going to take her hand. 'I just wanted to see if you were okay after last night. It must have been a shock seeing Jeremy like that.'

Jeremy! The mention of her ex's name bought tears to Gail's eyes, which she hadn't expected. Turning, she tried to brush them away but Paul had noticed.

'You're upset,' he said gently. 'I get that. I really do. Maybe there's still unfinished business between the two of you. To be honest, looking at the man's face, I'd say he was still in love with you ...'

'Don't!' Gail rounded on him. 'Jeremy Lord doesn't even know the meaning of the word! I've made a new start for myself and I don't want him messing up my life again. Look, Paul. I know you mean well. But I never want to hear his name again. Is that clear?'

Too late, she realised she was actually snapping at her boss! The tables have turned, she reminded herself. Paul could get rid of her at a moment's notice if he wanted. Then she'd have to find a new job. 'I'm sorry,' she said. 'I didn't mean to speak to you like that.'

'We're old friends,' Paul said. 'I'm glad that you can.'

Was it her imagination or had he changed from the rather difficult Paul she used to know at the airline. Maybe it was she who had changed ... Really! It was all so confusing.

'Changing the subject,' she said, still with a catch in her throat, 'could we discuss this idea I had for the hotel reception area?'

'Sure.' He pulled up a chair. 'I'm all ears.'

***

Thank goodness for work, Gail told herself as she headed home that night. There was nothing like it for distraction. Maybe that's where her future lay. As a single career woman. That way she wouldn't get her heart broken again.

'That you, Gail?' called out a voice from the kitchen.

Mmmm. Something smelt good!

Her dad was flipping over a piece of steak in a pan. 'There's something I need to tell you.'

'Why do I have a bad feeling about this?' asked Gail, pulling up a chair.

He patted her on the back. 'And why do you always assume the worst when I say we need to chat?'

'Experience,' muttered Gail.

Either he hadn't heard or was pretending not to. 'Guess who I saw out jogging today?'

Gail reached over for the bottle of wine which Rob had clearly already started. 'Sorry. I don't feel up to guessing games.'

'Jeremy.'

Gail spluttered. 'What?'

Rob had the grace to look slightly embarrassed. 'Out jogging, he was, in the park. So I told him to leave you alone. Don't look like that. I was furious when you told me what happened in the restaurant last night. Anyway, he said that he was actually coming to see me with some good news.'

Gail could hardly believe her ears. 'Whatever it is, you can't believe him. That man doesn't know how to tell the truth.'

'Just hear me out. Please. Anyway, we went to the coffee shop and he bought me a slap up breakfast ...'

'Bribery.'

'Gail! Let me tell you the whole story. Jeremy told me that he'd got Number 13 back.'

'Number 13?' whispered Gail. Her skin broke out into cold goosebumps. 'No. Please tell me that's not true.'

'So I told him straight.' Rob topped up his own glass. 'I said, "Jeremy, I don't want to get mixed up with you again after what happened with my daughter".'

'Thank you,' murmured Gail. Then she caught sight of her dad's face. 'Wait a minute. You went back on your word, didn't you?'

'Well, I nearly didn't ...'

Gail groaned.

'But you've got to admit it ... well, he's got something.'

'So you let him persuade you to get involved,' said Gail slowly.

'Smart girl.'

'Smarter than you, obviously. I don't know how you can do that, Dad. You know I don't want him in my life any more.'

'But you were husband and wife once, Gail. It's not that easy. And anyway, you *know* what a weakness I have for a project like this.'

All too true! Meanwhile, there was something else she needed to bring up. Gail cast a look at the engine parts which were strewn around the patio. Dad was always bringing something home to work on. 'When are you going to clear this lot up? We had another complaint from the neighbours the other day.'

'Ah.' Rob was still looking awkward. 'That's the other thing. I'm afraid I've got some more news which isn't quite so good …'

***

PAUL

'So it turns out that Dad's being kicked out of his place because the neighbours have complained about him.' Gail and Paul were sitting in the hotel bar, having a quick catch up meeting. It was meant to be about her idea for improving the staff rota but the subject had quickly changed to something more personal.

'It's not just the noise and car parts.' She sighed. 'It's his general behaviour. You know what Dad can be like if he doesn't think much of someone.'

'Unsociable?' suggested Paul.

'That's understating it. They want him out by the end of next week. That means I haven't got anywhere to live either.' She looked down at the bar, feeling awkward about what she had to say next. 'The thing is, Paul, I was wondering if the company has anything. I know it's short notice but it would give me some time to look for something else.'

'Really sorry but we're full up at the moment.'

She knew it. She shouldn't have asked. It made her look vulnerable. As if she couldn't cope on her own. Hadn't she told herself after Jeremy that she'd never rely on anyone else again; not even a friend?

'But I have heard that Number 22 in Ramsay Street is coming up. Clive, who owns it – do you know him? – wants to rent it out.'

'Really?' Gail looked up, excitedly. She was even more lovely when her face lit up like that. 'Great!'

'And it's big enough for both you and your dad.'

'Hah! We'll see about that. In fact, I think I've got an idea.' She glanced at her watch. 'Listen, do you mind if I knock off a bit early to find Clive?'

'Sure. You put in enough overtime with Mr Udagawa. I really appreciate it. This deal is more important than I can say.'

'Well, I'll do my best to play my part. He's having a bit of a rest for the next couple of days and then it's back to some more sightseeing.' Gail reached out and squeezed Paul's hand. Then she quickly withdrew it. 'Really grateful for the tip off about Number 22.'

'It's a pleasure.'

The touch of her hand just then had been unexpected. She looked embarrassed now as if she hadn't meant it. It took him right back to the time at the airline when they'd kissed. It had happened almost without him meaning to after a staff party. That had led to those two or three dates which had convinced him there was nothing in it apart from a brief physical attraction. Now he couldn't help liking Gail – although not in *that* way.

But it was awkward. She was going to be his family's neighbour. In some ways, that might be tricky as they were also working together. You needed to draw a line between the office and home life. But on the other hand, it could be fun having her a few doors down the street from the Robinsons …

***

GAIL

All sorted! Gail felt really excited as she walked over to Dad's garage. He'd be pleased too about their new home. And it would also be a good bargaining chip …

'Gail!' said Rob, looking up from a car bonnet. He didn't seem very happy to see her. And it was obvious why.

Blood rushed to her head as she took in the other man standing next to him. 'What are you doing here?'

'Hi, Gail. Nice to see you too.' Jeremy ran a hand over the cooler tank. 'Just giving your dad a chance to look at this little beauty here.'

Number 13. The car was pretty amazing all right, with that low-slung green body, stylish contour and huge racing wheels. But it also spelt danger. 'Well, you can stop right there. Don't you get it, Dad? This car is jinxed. Jeremy's father was killed in it. It hurts everyone it comes into contact with. But you've fallen for it, haven't you? I reckon this car means more to you than I do!'

Rob moved towards her, arms outstretched. 'Of course it doesn't. But Jeremy's right. She is a beauty. Right now, she's a sleeping princess, just waiting to be woken up.'

'You're crazy,' she retorted, stepping away. 'Both of you.'

'Look, Gail. I know I've given you a hard time in the past and I'm sorry.'

Gail snorted.

'But the thing is,' continued Jeremy, 'that Number 13 meant everything to my dad. And once I get her back on the circuit I can show everyone what she's capable of.'

'Don't give me this rubbish. You know what? I actually came over here to tell you I've found a new place for us to live in. But if you're dead set on bringing Jeremy and this ... this thing back into our lives, then I'll move in on my own. Got it?'

Then, ignoring both men's shocked faces, she turned on her heels and walked out.

***

PAUL

He was working late in the office when Gail came in. To his dismay, he could see she was crying.

'What's wrong?'

Tearfully, Gail explained the situation.

'But why shouldn't your dad get involved? Cars are what he does, after all.'

'Because Dad, Jeremy and Jeremy's father put everything into that wretched thing – and we all paid the price. We hardly saw them. It took over their lives. Then there was the crash and Jeremy's dad ... he was killed instantly. I don't want anything to do with it. It's nothing but bad luck.'

Paul handed her a coffee. 'Do you really believe in that sort of thing?'

Before she had a chance to answer, there was a knock on the door. 'Thought I might find you here.'

It was Rob.

'Dad. Please. Go away.'

'I just wanted to tell you something. After you stormed off, Jim came in. He loved the car too. He's really interested in helping out as well. And as for the new place, well, I'd really like to take a look if that's all right.'

What a cheek! 'I told you before. It's the car or me. Take it on and you can't move in with me.'

'You don't really mean that do you?'

'Yes, I do.'

'Maybe,' said Paul gently, 'it wouldn't do any harm to let your dad take a look at the place. You've got the keys, haven't you?'

He glanced at Gail. Hopefully she could see what he was thinking – that her father might change his mind when he realised what he had to lose. 'I might have made mistakes,' Paul told himself, 'but I hope I'm a loyal friend.' All he wanted was to make sure that things worked out for Gail. Her distress really upset him. She'd been through so much with that rat of a husband Jeremy. The man had a lot to answer for.

***

GAIL

'So how are you enjoying the new job?' asked Helen, offering her the plate of biscuits.

Gail took a chocolate biccy out of politeness. It had been really kind of Helen to ask her to coffee at Number 26 but she really wasn't feeling hungry or particularly sociable. Not after everything that had been going on.

'I love it,' she said truthfully.

'I know Paul's very pleased with your ideas. I said you'd be the right person for the job.'

'Thanks. You've all been so kind at making me feel at

home.' It was true. Even though Gail hadn't initially wanted company today, Helen was so easy to talk to. In a funny way, she was also a bit of a mother figure in her life although, of course, no one could ever replace Mum.

'It's a pleasure. Talking of home, I gather you've had a few issues.' Helen smiled kindly at Gail. 'Maybe that's why you seem so quiet today.'

'I'm so sorry.' Gail put down her coffee mug. 'Forgive me for not being much company. But the truth is that I feel really uncomfortable now Jeremy is back. He and Dad are going ahead with the car. And I ... well I went back on my threat to say he couldn't live with me if he did.'

'I heard as much from Paul.'

'The thing is that it clearly means so much to Dad. But I'm worried.' Gail hesitated, wondering whether to mention her jinxed theory to Helen. Maybe not. She might think she was crazy. 'The repairs are going to be really expensive and, frankly, I doubt whether Jeremy will ever pay Dad. He's good at getting things out of people for nothing. I've told Dad I don't want him to talk about the car when he's round me. And I certainly don't want him talking about that ex-husband of mine.'

Helen reached out her hand. 'This Jeremy must have hurt you very much.'

'Yes. He did. It's been eighteen months now but it still ... well, it still hurts.'

'I hear he's quite a charmer.' Helen shook her head. 'Men like that can be hard to get out of your head.'

'Well I don't want him there any more.'

Helen briefly put her hand over hers. 'Then tell him. In my experience, men often need things to be spelled out. Make it clear.'

'I thought I had.'

'So there's not much more you can do, is there? Now how about a slice of my strawberry gateau? It's a new recipe and I've been dying to try it out!'

***

'Not much more you can do.'

Helen's words rang round her head as Gail walked back home. Was that true? Maybe she should have one more go. Almost without meaning to, Gail found her feet walking towards the hotel. 'I just want to check something in the register,' she told the receptionist. There it was. Jeremy's room number. It looked as though he was out. But the spare key was on the rack.

Her heart beating, Gail made her way to the fourth floor and let herself in. Was she going mad? Curiously, she looked around.

Jeremy was clearly as untidy as he'd always been. There was his blue shirt draped over the chair: the same shirt she'd bought him two years ago for his birthday. Not knowing why, Gail went across and held it to her face. It smelt just like him. Then she flung it down. Why couldn't she get this man out of her mind? Was it possible that she didn't really want to?

The key turned in the door. 'Gail!' Jeremy's face was a picture of disbelief and – yes – pleasure. 'What are you doing here? I mean, it's great to see you but you've taken me by surprise.'

'Why? Have you got a girlfriend in tow?'

'Of course not.' He came close to her. She stepped away. 'But we *are* divorced. You remember that.'

'Oh yes. I remember all right.'

'Drink?' He indicated the drinks cupboard. 'Pink gin? Or have you gone off that now?'

So he remembered.

'I've come to tell you something.'

'Really? Please sit down. Cheers! To the old times.'

He looked so self-confident. So sure of himself.

'I've come to say that I don't want you back in my life. Things are going really well and you aren't going to ruin them for me again.'

Instantly, his face expressed regret. 'Look, Gail. I haven't come here to do that. I promise that your dad's involvement with Number 13 doesn't mean I'll be getting in your way.'

Gail put down her drink. 'Really? We're bound to bump into each other all the time with Dad working with you.'

'Wouldn't that be nice?'

This was quite enough.

'No. It wouldn't.'

She got up to go. What was he doing?

'Don't you dare try to kiss me!'

Raising her hand, she slapped him before stepping back, horrified at what she'd done. But Jeremy just smiled at her.

'That's my Gail. You've just proved what I've always suspected.'

'What's that?' she whispered.

'That you still care for me. Otherwise you wouldn't be so upset.'

'Rubbish!'

'Is it? Then why are you here?'

'Not for any longer.' Then she turned on her heels and marched out of the room. Only when she reached the street, did Gail begin to run. Tears streaming down her face.

Eight

GAIL

'Honestly, love. I don't think you should get mixed up with Jeremy again.'

They were standing outside the door of Number 22 Ramsay Street after all their stuff had been unloaded. It had been exhausting! And frankly the last thing Gail needed was a conversation about the man who had ruined her life.

'Mixed up?' repeated Gail, feeling a wave of indignation pass through her. 'Don't you get it, Dad? I've asked him to leave Erinsborough.'

He was looking at her closely. 'So why do I get the feeling you didn't really mean it? You're my daughter. I know you better than you think.'

This was too much. 'And I'm old enough to know my own mind too.'

Rob nodded. 'You certainly are.' He glanced at their new home. 'And you've come up trumps with this place. Thanks for letting me tag along with you.'

'Come on.' Gail gave him a quick hug. 'You know I wouldn't leave you in the lurch. Anyway, it's Paul who gave me the heads up on the house. We've got him to thank.'

'And here comes the man himself!'

Gail pretended to busy herself with some weeds that needed pulling out by the front door.

'We were just singing your praises, mate. This place is perfect.'

'Glad I could help.' Paul was speaking to her dad but his eyes were on her. 'Everything all right?'

Gail was beginning to regret calling him after leaving Jeremy's room. But she'd needed someone to confide in …

'Why shouldn't it be?'

Her words came out sharper than she'd meant.

Paul was looking awkward now. 'You know. Jeremy. I just … well I don't want you getting hurt again.'

'Please! Will everyone stop treating me like a child. Now if the two of you don't mind, I've got a house to sort out. Everything's in a right old mess and I've only got the weekend to get our stuff unpacked before I start work again.'

'You can have some time off if you need it.'

'No thanks. I wasn't asking for favours. Look, don't take this the wrong way, Paul, but I need some space. Dad? Are you going to give me a hand or are you going to stand there all day and discuss my love life – or rather lack of it? And by the way, I hope you're going to get on with the new neighbours better than you did with the last lot.'

Paul patted Rob on the back. 'Don't think we'll have

any problems with that. Nearly forgot to mention something, Gail. Gran wondered if you'd like to pop in and say hello. Might give you a bit of a break with all the unpacking, don't you think?'

**

She really didn't have time but it would look rude not to accept the invitation. After all, the Robinsons were only next door but one. But even if they hadn't been, she'd have made friends with Helen. Not only was she nice but she was also intelligent and a good listener.

In fact, Gail found herself saying far more than she'd meant to partly because it was such a relief to talk it through, woman to woman. 'I was really flattered when Jeremy first showed an interest in me.' Her voice grew dreamy. 'He was handsome, charming and ... well ... he could have had his pick of women.'

'But he chose *you* which made you feel important,' said Helen.

Gail nodded ruefully. 'Exactly. But after we got married, he ... well things changed very quickly.' She pressed her lips together trying to shut out the pain. 'I found evidence of affairs. Several of them.'

The older woman's hand reached out to touch hers. 'I'm sorry. That must have been awful for you.'

Gail took a sip of tea to try and calm herself. The memories were flooding back now, rather like an old wound bursting open. 'I finally told him that I couldn't go on like this and that our marriage was over but he's such an egomaniac he didn't believe me. After our divorce, he began sending me postcards of places we'd been to. And then the other evening he turned up at

Lassiters when I was having a business dinner with Paul.'

'Maybe,' said Helen softly, 'he thought you and Paul were together.'

'He's my boss!'

'I know that, dear, but relationships can be complicated.'

'Paul and I are good friends now. Far more than when we were at the airline together. Besides, I … well … I went round to Jeremy's hotel room to tell him to stay away. And he … he kissed me.'

Helen was holding her hand even tighter now. 'Did you feel anything for him?'

'That's just it.' Gail could feel a tear trickling down her cheek. 'I told him to go away but, despite everything, I still love him. And now I just don't know what to do.'

***

How stupid of her, Gail told herself the following day. What if Helen told Paul? She said she wouldn't but Helen was Paul's gran after all and blood was thicker than water. Then again, so what if she did? It wasn't as though Gail felt anything for Paul. More that she didn't want her affairs to be known. Which was exactly why she shouldn't have confided in Helen in the first place …

'Just follow your heart but make sure that it sees sense at the same time,' the older woman had advised.

How on earth did you do that?

'Hi! The door was open. 'Hope you didn't mind me coming in.'

For a minute, Gail had to do a double-take. She was

so used to seeing Paul in his office clothes that she almost didn't recognise him in T-shirt and shorts.

Nice legs! Muscly without being fat. Manly hairs too! Then she caught herself. What was she thinking of?

His face looked serious. 'I've got something to tell you actually.'

So Helen had told him.

'She had no right …'

'Guess who I bumped into last night in the hotel …'

How embarrassing! They'd both started to talk at the same time.

'*Who* had no right?' asked Paul confused.

'No one.' Gail felt herself blushing. 'I got muddled for a minute. Who did you bump into?'

Paul's voice was steady. As if he was worried about showing too much emotion. 'Your ex.'

Gail was still trying to get her head round this when Paul spoke again. 'He congratulated me on us getting together.'

She gasped. 'What?'

Paul shrugged. 'Clearly he'd got the wrong idea about us. I explained we just had a working relationship and then he insisted that I came into his room for a drink. It seemed wrong not to. Bit of a smoothie, isn't he?'

Gail sat down heavily on the chair which she'd just positioned by the window. 'Oh yes.'

'Got the feeling that he was probing me for details about you too. Then he asked if the Daniels Corporation would like to sponsor his racing car. Reckoned it would be good publicity for the company!'

'How dare he!' Gail grabbed Paul's arm almost without realising it. 'That car is jinxed. Please don't get involved with it.'

'Don't look so worried. I'm having nothing to do with it.'

'That's a relief.'

'Glad you approve. Listen, there's something else too.'

Hadn't she had enough news for one day?

'Mr Udagawa is in town as you know and I've promised to take him out. So Gran suggested we invited him round for another family evening. Look – I know you've done more than your fair share but would you mind coming round and doing a bit of entertaining as well. It would really help to clinch the deal.'

'Sure.' Anything, thought Gail privately, to keep her mind off that kiss with Jeremy.

***

The evening went far better than Gail had expected. Most of the conversation centred around their respective families. Their guest produced even more photographs of his children, while Helen and Jim made them all laugh with stories about Paul as a little boy. 'Remember how he got his foot stuck in the chair that Christmas and we had to saw him out?' said Helen.

Jim covered his eyes. 'As if I could forget.'

'What a lovely man,' commented Helen as Gail helped her tidy up while Paul took Mr Udagawa back to the hotel.

'Fancies himself as a matchmaker, too!' added Jim with a wink. 'While you ladies were out in the kitchen, he kept telling me what a fine couple Paul and Gail would make!'

Gail laughed. 'He's said as much to me.'

'Who, Paul?'

'No.' She playfully flicked Jim on the shoulder. 'Mr Udagawa!'

It was late when Gail got home. Goodness she could do with bed! But just as she was about to undress and take a shower, the phone rang.

'Gail?'

It was Jeremy.

'Please. Don't hang up on me. I want to talk. About us.'

'And I don't.'

'I can't stop thinking about you.' He continued as if she hadn't spoken, just as he used to when they were married. 'I miss you, Gail.'

I miss you too, she wanted to say. But it wouldn't work. Would it? He only wanted her now because she was playing cool. If she agreed to start again, he'd go back to his old ways. Slowly, she forced herself to hang up.

The doorbell! Surely that couldn't be Jeremy. Not so soon after the call. Then again, when he wanted something, he never gave up.

'I told you just now,' she began ... then stopped.

'I'm sorry.' It was Paul. Still wearing his smart clothes from earlier that evening. 'Look I know it's late. But there's something I need to tell you before you see Mr Udagawa tomorrow.'

Gail had never seen Paul look so nervous before. What was going on?

'Our client says he prefers to do business with, as he puts it, "family men".' He shifted from one foot to another in the small hallway. 'So I ... well, I told him that we are getting married.'

'Who's "we"?'

'Er, you and me.'

'WHAT?'

The idea was so ridiculous that Gail burst out laughing.

'Look, it's not as crazy as it sounds. Mind if we sit down?'

Stunned, she led him into the lounge room.

'Listen, we've got more in common than maybe we thought at first. We're both ambitious. If we get married, we can help each other reach our goals.'

Gail could hardly believe what she was hearing. 'You make it sound like a business proposal.'

'Well, in a way it is.'

Weren't a lot of marriages based on convenience? She just never saw herself as being part of such an arrangement. Mind you, she should have seen this coming. Paul was very hard-headed when it came to business. She'd seen that already. And Gail had been quite shocked when Jane had let slip about Paul complaining he wasn't a charity worker when two women had wanted to job-share the post before she'd got it. How awful was that? Then again, it wasn't as though getting married for love had worked out for her before. So maybe Paul did have a point. Yet she still had a flutter of misgiving. Wasn't it like getting married on false pretences?

'I get what you mean,' said Paul when she explained this. 'But our marriage will stand a better chance without all that complicated emotional stuff. Haven't we both been hurt that way before? Instead, we'll be going into this with our eyes open, and that means we can support each other. What do you think?'

'I think,' said Gail weakly, 'I need a coffee. Want one?'

'Please.'

He followed her into the kitchen. 'Just think about it. Quickly, before tomorrow. You won't have to worry about hassle from creeps like Jeremy if I'm your husband.'

'Fine. Are you going to put that in our vows?'

'Don't be like that. We could always divorce if it doesn't work out.'

'What a charmer. You're really selling this!'

'It's a big deal, Gail. We could lose it if you don't agree. And it could really help both of us at the same time.'

Gail handed him a small mug. Not too big or he might spend even longer drinking it. Right now she needed to be alone. 'Let me think about it.'

'So it's not a "no" then?'

'I said I need to mull it over. But I'll give you an answer in the morning.' Their hands touched briefly as she reached over for her own mug. 'I promise.'

***

'Do you take this man to be your wedded husband ...'

'STOP! I'm not sure. Yes. No.'

Gail sat bolt upright in bed, her chest pounding. It took a few seconds to realise she'd been dreaming. What a relief! She hadn't been getting married at all. But who exactly had she been about to marry in her dream? Try as she might, Gail just couldn't picture the groom's face.

That was when she remembered. This morning was when she'd promised to tell Paul if she'd go along with his crazy idea.

'Morning, love.' Rob looked up from his toast. 'Slept well, did you?'

'Sort of.'

He reached across for the butter even though he already had more than enough on his slice. 'Thought I heard voices here last night. Had a visitor, did you?'

'If you mean Jeremy, the answer's no. It was just Paul. He needed to ask me something.'

'Pretty late to discuss business matters wasn't it?'

'It was urgent. Actually he asked me to marry him.'

Rob began to choke. 'You're kidding, right? No? That's absolutely brilliant. I always knew he was the right man for you.' Leaping up from his chair, he gave her a big bear hug. 'Love, I can't tell you how pleased I am.'

Gail was putting the kettle on. 'Just joking, Dad.'

His face fell. 'Really?'

'I told you before. I'm never getting married again. Well not in the foreseeable future anyway.'

'I see.' He stuffed the rest of the toast into his mouth and got up. 'Well thanks for disappointing me. I'm off to the workshop now to work on that little beauty.'

'You mean Jeremy's car?'

'I certainly do.'

'How could you, Dad?'

Gail turned on her heels.

'Where are you going?'

'Where do you think? To see the man who got us into all this trouble in the first place.'

Just then the phone rang.

'Gail?' It was Helen.

'Something weird has happened. Mr Udagawa has just turned up with a bonsai tree. He said it was an engagement present for you and Paul. Am I missing something here?'

'Look, I'm sorry Helen but I can't talk right now. Can I come round and see you later? I'll explain then.'

This was going to be awkward, Gail told herself. How was she going to talk her way out of this one?

***

'Fancy seeing you here, Gail.'

She had a feeling that Jeremy would be hanging around the garage. And she was right.

'Dad told me about the car,' she said, launching straight in.

'Ah, that.' He made one of those 'come on, Gail' faces. 'For a moment there, I thought you'd come to say that you'll accept my invitation after all.'

'You must be kidding – especially as you've talked Dad into working on Number 13. I've told you before. It's bad luck. I just know it.'

Jeremy sighed. 'I'm not dragging him into anything. I can't keep him away. He's like a kid with a new toy. Listen, why don't you have lunch with me? If, at the end, you decide you really never want to see me again, I promise to keep away.'

'Honestly?'

'Cross my heart.'

'All right. But I've got a meeting this afternoon. So it will have to be twelve. At the hotel restaurant.'

'Thanks, Gail.' For a minute she thought he was going to try and kiss her again. Instead, he raised her hand to his mouth in an old-fashioned gesture which was oddly – and irritatingly – touching. 'You won't regret it.'

***

Gail was in the Ladies when she heard the conversation outside by the washbasins. It was Helen's voice.

'I tell you – I can hardly believe it myself. There we were – Jim, Scott and I – and Paul comes in through the back door. Mr Udagawa has just left after delivering the bonsai tree. So we ask him straight. Paul? Is it true? Are you really engaged to Gail? Then he says he's sorry that Mr Udagawa got in there first with the news and that he's realised how he feels about Gail! Of course, we all gave him a big hug. I did ask him if he was certain Gail was over her ex-husband and he assured me that she was.'

This was awful! Who was Helen talking to? Now everyone would know! How dare Paul? She hadn't even given him her decision.

Then there was the sound of the door opening. Gail could only just catch Helen's voice. 'Don't tell anyone? Promise?'

Hah! That rumour wouldn't take long to get round. Meanwhile, she was due to have lunch with Jeremy in half an hour. Maybe, instead of going back to her office, she'd just sneak out and arrive a bit early. There was no way Gail wanted to face those curious faces right now.

To her surprise, Jeremy was already waiting. At first he didn't see her. Gail's heart gave a little jump. There was something about him – despite his appalling behaviour – that always made her do that. Since the divorce, she'd felt as though only half of her was here. The rest was with

Jeremy. By his side. Would it always be like that? Or would she, one day, grow out of yearning for this handsome impossible man who had broken her heart?

'Gail!'

His eyes took in her face and then skirted over her body and back again to her face. 'You look absolutely stunning as usual.'

'Thank you.' She spoke crisply, not wanting to give him any ideas. It certainly wouldn't do if he knew about the confusion whirling round her head.

'Tell me about your morning.'

Jeremy was trying hard. She'd give him that. He rarely asked her about anything. In the past it had always been him, him, him! When the waiter came to take their order, she chose the most expensive dish on the menu: lobster thermidor. Jeremy – who had always been quite tight during their marriage when it had come to money – didn't bat an eyelid.

'Good choice. Think I'll have the same. And your best bottle of champagne, please.'

'You've changed,' Gail couldn't resist saying.

'I have.' Jeremy's eyes held hers. 'You know what they say?'

He was flirting with her! Just like he used to in the old days. 'What do they say?'

'That it takes a good woman to do that.' Then he raised his glass and clinked it against hers. 'I've missed you, Gail. You're the only woman who has got my measure. And you know what? I reckon I'm the only bloke who gets you too. Now let's have a bit of fun, shall we?'

***

Either Jeremy really *had* changed or she'd misunderstood him. Either way, she'd had a great time, and told him so as he drove her home.

'Really?'

They were standing in her lounge room. Close. Very close. Move away, Gail told herself. But she couldn't.

'I know you still love me,' he said quietly. Then he leant forward and kissed her.

'No,' she moaned but his lips were hard on hers.

It was no good. Try as she did, she just couldn't resist. Then a picture flashed into her head. The lipstick mark round a wine glass when she'd come home early from work one night. One more piece of evidence that Jeremy had been playing around. Leopards don't change their spots.

'I don't want this,' she said, breaking away.

'I think you do.'

'No! I can't. You hurt me too much. The affairs. The arguments – just like we're having now over that damned car.'

'Is that what this is about? Okay, if it means so much to you, I'll sell it.'

'What?'

'I mean it. Really.'

Gail was so shocked she didn't know what to say. When Jeremy kissed her again, she didn't try to stop him.

'Gail!'

'Dad?'

Instantly she sprang apart from Jeremy.

'I have to say, I'm surprised to see you here.' Rob was glowering at Jeremy. 'You do realise that my Gail is engaged to Paul Robinson, don't you?'

'That can't be true.' Jeremy's voice was like thunder. 'You're making it up because you don't approve of me.' Then he turned to Gail. 'Isn't he?'

She could hardly bear to look him in the face.

'Calm down. Please. It's complicated. Let me try to explain …'

Nine

PAUL

Paul was knee-deep in a pile of figures when the office door opened. If he could persuade these suppliers to take the low offer he'd suggested, he was really onto a winner! Of course, it helped that the company in question was desperate for his business. The directors were all mortgaged up to the hilt. Still that wasn't his problem.

'I thought I said I wasn't to be disturbed,' he said without looking up.

'Your secretary wasn't around so I let myself in.'

Paul could hardly believe his eyes. 'What are you doing here? Don't you believe in knocking?'

Jeremy took the chair opposite without so much as a 'by your leave'. 'Not as much as you believe in deception, mate.'

Great. Paul knew exactly what was coming.

Jeremy leant forward. 'Let me make myself clear. Gail's told me about this sham engagement of yours and

I won't stand for it.'

What cheek! 'It's got nothing to do with you.'

'Actually, it has.' A self-satisfied smile crept across his face. 'Gail and I are back together again.'

'I don't believe it.'

'Ask her then. The thing is, mate, I need money for Number 13. And you are going to sponsor me. Otherwise, I'll make sure Gail backs out of this arrangement of yours, and I'll tell Udagawa the whole sorry story.'

'That's blackmail!'

Jeremy shrugged. 'I wouldn't put it quite like that.'

'I thought you said you wouldn't put up with our engagement just now.'

There was another shrug. 'Not unless you cough up the money, mate.'

'Will you stop calling me "mate". Now get out.'

'Okay, Okay, I'm going. No need to push me like that.'

'I want you out of the hotel as well. Got it?'

Jeremy stood at the door, both hands in his pockets. He looked for all the world as though he owned this place and not Paul. 'Be careful what you say, Paul. You might need my help one day. More than you realise.'

What the hell did he mean by that?

No sooner had the door closed than Paul grabbed the phone to call Gail at the catering convention she was attending at the other end of town.

'Paul? Can you hear me? Sorry – there's a lot of noise at this end.'

'I wanted to talk to you,' said Paul grimly.

Her voice babbled with excitement. 'Me too. Look,

I've just met someone who might be useful in promoting that idea I had for the hotel about ...'

'Forget that. Your ex-husband has just turned up. Did you know he was coming?'

'Sorry. I can't hear you properly. This place is packed. *Who's* turned up?'

'Just come back to the office,' he shouted down the line. 'As fast as you can. Forget networking. This is more important.'

While he was waiting, Paul went back to his figures. But none of them made sense. All he could think about was that damned man. How could Gail trust him – and what the hell did she see in him?

At last, he heard her footsteps clattering across the corridor outside. He'd recognise them anywhere. His heart began to beat with nerves as though he was a teenager again.

'Are you all right?'

Her face was pink as if she'd been running. It suited her. In fact, thought Paul with a start, Gail was one of those women who grew more beautiful as she got older rather than less so.

Quickly he explained. 'Can you believe it? *Blackmail*. Please tell me you're not really reconciled. Surely you haven't been taken in by him and his phony act?'

As soon as the words came out of his mouth, he realised he'd said the wrong thing.

'I'm quite capable of making my own decisions, thank you very much.'

'I know that but ...'

Gail cut in. 'Look, I'm not saying he was right. In fact, he was very wrong to try and make you sponsor him. But as for what is and isn't between him and me, that's none of your business. So if you don't mind, I'm going back to the convention. And I'd be grateful if you only contacted me for business reasons in future. Not personal.'

She was talking as if she was the boss again, back at the airline. But this time it was different. This time it wasn't his pride which was hurting. It was his heart.

Paul reached for the phone. There was one person who might just understand. Someone who, despite his other faults, was (on the whole) sensible, kind and level-headed.

'It's me. Look, have you got time to meet up? Somewhere quiet where we can talk.'

***

Jim suggested a small café by the library. 'I come in here sometimes with my books.'

Paul did a double-take. 'But you're not much of a reader.'

'Maybe not when you were a kid. But over the years, I've found it helps me relax.' Jim patted the pile next to him. 'Non-fiction. None of your romantic stuff, mind you. I've had enough of that.'

Paul rubbed his eyes. Suddenly he felt very tired. 'Me too. Or so I thought.'

'It's Gail, isn't it.' Jim's face turned almost soft. 'Come on then, son. Tell me what's up?'

'Look, Dad, the truth is that Gail and I have had a bit of a row about something. But I don't want to go into details. It wouldn't be fair on her.'

'Not easy.' Paul's dad clapped him on the back in

sympathy and breathed out a big sigh. 'But I think I know what the problem is. Like many others who've been married before, you're finding it hard to move on with someone else – no matter how difficult the first marriage was. But you don't need me to remind you of that after your experience.'

Paul pretended to stir his coffee so he didn't have to look his dad in the face.

'If you want my advice, it's not to push things. Don't tell Gail what she should or shouldn't do. Women don't like that any more. Just be there for her when she needs you. You young people are so good at making life complicated.' Jim patted his shoulder. 'But you never know. This might turn out for the best. You're just going to have to wait and see.'

'Thanks.' Paul was toying with the sugar now. 'You're right. Just what I was thinking really but it's good to have a second opinion.'

Jim rubbed his eyes. Then yawned.

'You okay? You seem a bit tired.'

'To be honest, I've had a few issues of my own. Lucy's back from France.'

'She is? But I thought she wasn't due home for a bit longer.'

Jim made a wry face. 'That's the problem. I felt she'd been there long enough so I made her come home. Now she's furious with me. She keeps going on about how amazing Europe is. You should see the clothes she's bought. Clearly Erinsborough isn't good enough for her now. Boring, apparently.'

That was Lucy! Always wanting something else.

It was Jim's turn now to stir his coffee and not look

him in the face. 'Says she'll never forgive me for making her come back early. Your gran's done her best to make her see sense. But I'm not sure that's going to happen any time soon. We can't match up to the British royal family.' He tapped a book next to him. 'She brought this back for me. Just to rub my nose in it.'

'What's that poking out?' Paul pointed to a piece of paper.

'Helen made her write me a note to say sorry.'

'That's something.'

'Not if she doesn't mean it.' Jim faced him fair and square. 'It's what we were saying earlier. You've got to talk from the heart when it comes to relationships. No point in pretending. Or hiding. Do you get what I mean?'

'Yes.' Paul nodded. 'I do. But it's not easy, is it?'

'No one said it was, son. All we can do is try. Now how about a beer? I think we both need one.'

***

Paul couldn't sleep. Why did family have to be so complicated? Why couldn't he have a nice quiet life? Then again, 'quiet' didn't seem to go with Gail's personality. Or his. They'd had so much fun last night when they had gone round to Dad and Gran's for dinner. To his relief, she'd put their argument behind them and had gone along with the game of charades which Lucy had suggested. They were mad keen on it in England apparently. Gail was brilliant! She'd got more points than anyone else. Maybe the engagement idea hadn't been so crazy after all. At times, he found himself wishing it was for real …

***

Paul spent the whole of the next day polishing up his final presentation to the suppliers. Looked like they were on the brink of accepting his very low offer. Great! That was the thing about business. There was nothing like going in for the kill! Mind you, it took it out of you. So on Sunday, he had a long swim to clear his head. By the time he got to Number 26, it was nearly lunch.

'Paul?' called out Helen when he was getting the barbie going. 'There's someone to see you.'

If Jeremy had the cheek to show his face here, he'd …

'Gail. Great to see you. Take a seat.'

How pretty she looked in that yellow dress. He wanted to say so but was worried she'd take it the wrong way. You never knew how Gail was going to react but it was part of her appeal.

'I need to fill you in on a few things.'

'This sounds serious.'

'It is. Sort of.'

'Would you like something to drink first?'

He indicated the jug of iced tea on the table.

'No thanks. I can't be long.'

This definitely didn't feel good.

'Jeremy came round for breakfast yesterday.'

'Came round or stayed over?'

Her voice hardened. 'Came round but even if he had stayed the night, it's none of your business. Do you want to hear what happened or not?'

He nodded. Maybe it was better to stay silent.

'I asked him about that so-called blackmail threat and he says you got it wrong. It was all a misunderstanding.'

'Is that right?'

'No need to sound so sarcastic. He just wants to be

friends with you. Especially as ...'

Her voice wavered.

'Especially what?'

'Well ...' Here Gail toyed with an imaginary thread on her dress. Paul knew that trick. She used to do the same with her airline uniform. 'He wanted to move in with me and Dad – so he can save on hotel bills and put the money towards the car.'

What? 'You're not going to agree?'

'I told him that Dad wouldn't go for it. Not now you and I are getting married.'

She gave a half-smile.

'And is that the only reason you turned him down?'

Gail ignored the question. 'Afterwards, Jeremy went over to the garage to look at the car. It's going to cost more than they thought ...'

'That's a surprise.'

'Paul!'

'Sorry.'

'And so he asked Dad about moving in.'

'That man's doesn't give up, does he?'

Gail sighed. 'I know it doesn't look good but, well, I kind of feel sorry for him. He's down on his luck, Paul.'

'You told your father you'd agree, didn't you?'

She nodded. Paul felt sick.

'There's something else too.'

He knew it.

'I've lent Jeremy some money. Don't look like that. He needed it for work on the car, so he can sell it and ... and maybe get married.'

'To who?'

Gail went pink. 'He's changed. He's promised.

Jeremy actually told me I mean more to him than the car does.'

Paul stood up. 'And you believe him? Honestly Gail, I thought you'd have more sense than that.'

'I knew you wouldn't understand.'

'So why did you bother telling me?'

'Paul?'

It was a young girl with an elfin face coming into the backyard, looking rather pale and tired.

'What's going on, Paul? I was trying to rest but I heard voices.'

'Sorry.' Paul looked awkward. 'Gail and I were talking about work stuff.'

'Hi!' Lucy stared up at her. 'I love what you've done with your hair today!'

'I like yours too!'

'Really?'

How she'd have loved a little sister like this.

Then she threw a look at Paul. 'Could we catch up later and discuss this office matter then, do you think?'

He gave her a hard stare back. 'That depends. Frankly I think my own proposal is best. It's in everyone's interest. Don't you think?'

***

How can women be so stupid? Paul stared at the computer on his office desk the next day. Jeremy's payment for the hotel room had bounced. Then again, what had he expected?

'No problem,' said Gail coldly when he called her in. 'Put the payment through again. It will be okay then.'

Paul groaned. 'You mean you'll put some money in

for him. Can't you see what he's doing? The man's a freeloader.'

'And I'm trying to help out someone who goes back a long way. Anyway, all you're interested in is Mr Udagawa.'

Paul drummed his fingers on the desk in an attempt to keep calm. 'This deal is important – I'll give you that – but you mean more. I just want to make sure you're all right.'

He said the last part in a low voice. She only seemed to take in the first bit.

'I know the deal is important. That's why I'm going along with this. But any more of your criticism, Paul, and I'm out. Okay?'

She slammed the office door as she left.

'Paul?'

For a minute he thought she'd come back. But it was Jane.

'Everything all right?'

He nodded tersely. 'Couldn't be better.'

'Ready to dictate that letter now?'

He'd almost forgotten.

'By the way,' added Jane. 'Mr Udagawa has gone to Alice Springs for a break. He left a message. Said he didn't want to bother you and was happy to go on his own.'

That was something. It might give him more time in case …

'And another thing!'

The door swung open. It was Gail – back again!

Out of the corner of his eye, Paul saw Jane diplomatically leave.

'I'm fed up of you thinking you know what's best for me. I'm calling off the engagement,' Gail fumed.

'You can't! We have an agreement.'

'Stuff that.' Her face was furious. 'Just count me out.'

'Gail! Please …'

His words fell on deaf ears. She was gone.

As Paul gripped the edge of the desk, his dad's words came back to him.

'If you want my advice, it's not to push things. Don't tell Gail what she should or shouldn't do. Women don't like that any more. Just be there for her when she needs you.'

But was it too late?

Ten

GAIL

There were some things you could never tire of, thought Gail, as she knelt on the grass next to the water's edge. Then she looked up at the man sitting next to her, his arm draped around her shoulder. Did that include people too? When she and Jeremy had broken up, she'd vowed that no one would ever break her heart again. But now, here she was …

'I'm so relieved you broke off that sham engagement with Paul.' Jeremy's voice sent tremors through her, just as it had always done. What was it about him that made her unable to resist?

Gail picked a blade of grass and twisted it round her little finger with nerves. 'I'm just worried that Paul will want to get back at me. He could fire me.'

'If he does, I'll have something to say to him.'

'No. Don't. Please.'

'Then maybe you should speak to him.' His hand began to stroke the top of her arm, bringing her skin out in tiny goosebumps. 'Can't you see he used you? It's time you did the same.'

Gail wriggled uncomfortably. 'That wouldn't feel right. But maybe you've got a point about talking to him frankly.' She moved away slightly to look him straight in the face. 'I believe in honesty, Jeremy.'

'So that's why you got engaged to a man you don't love – just to get a business deal?'

He had a point.

'That was a mistake but that's exactly why I ended it. Look, if we're going to move on, I need you to be honest too.'

Jeremy cupped her face in his hands. 'Listen to me, Gail. I've changed. I promise. If I could turn back the clock, believe me I would. In fact …'

Gail stood up quickly. Was he about to propose? No. Surely not. And if he was, what should she say? 'I'll speak to Paul now,' she said, grabbing her bag. 'But Dad's going out this evening. We can talk then.'

He was standing too now, close to her. 'I'd like that,' he said softly. Then he bent down and kissed her. It felt so right. So good. As if they had never been parted. Then he gave her a playful flick on the bottom. 'Go on then. Get things straight with the boss. See you later on.'

***

'Paul?'

The office was empty as you would expect on a Saturday. But she'd overheard Paul saying that he'd be at his desk most of the weekend to catch up. Thank goodness there wasn't anyone else around. This was awkward enough as it was. Somehow they'd both managed to avoid being alone together since she'd broken off the engagement but things couldn't go on like this.

'Hi.' Paul looked unsmiling. Gail's heart sank. 'Was there something you wanted to discuss with me?'

'Please. Don't be like that.'

'Don't be like what?'

'Can I sit down?'

He gestured to the chair without speaking.

'Look, I just want to know where we go from here ... well, after ... you know.'

'After you called off the engagement?'

'We both know the engagement wasn't serious.'

'I thought we had an arrangement.'

'We did but ... well it wouldn't have worked, would it? We were just kidding ourselves. Maybe it wasn't just because of Mr Udagawa. Perhaps we've both found ourselves at a lonely crossroads in life and felt we needed each other. But we're stronger than that, aren't we?'

'You certainly seem to be.' He was looking at her with a mixture of hurt and anger. Was it possible that she'd read him all wrong?

Her hands twisted the strap of her handbag just as they'd twisted the blade of grass by the water with Jeremy. 'Do I still have a job or not?'

'Of course you do.'

That was a relief!

'But it's not going to be easy, is it?' he added.

'We can smooth things over.' She was babbling, keen to get back to more even ground. 'You've got to tell Mr Udagawa that it's over. Blame me. Explain that I broke it off.'

Paul picked up a pen and started going through some

documents on his desk. 'If that's what you want.' Then he threw the papers across the desk, making her jump. 'Gail. What do you think you're doing, being taken in by that ex-husband of yours? Haven't you learned anything from the way he's treated you?'

This was enough! 'People change,' she snapped back. 'And anyway, it's none of your business.'

Oh dear, she thought, running to her car. Now she'd gone and made things even worse. How were she and Paul going to work together after this?

***

'Dad! You're back early. I'm so glad.'

Gail rushed into her father's arms.

'What's wrong, love?'

It felt so good to be held by him. For a minute, Gail felt like a little girl again, being comforted by her daddy.

'It's Paul. He's ... well he's being really horrible about me breaking off the engagement.'

Rob stepped back, holding her face, rather like Jeremy had held it a few hours earlier but in a kind, fatherly fashion. 'You can see why he's upset. A lovely girl like you. Any man would be proud to call you his own. That's why I've always been so protective of you. Look, if I were you, I'd sort things out with Paul fast. You've got to work with the man.'

'How did it go with boss man?'

It was Jeremy, walking in from the patio with a glass of beer in his hand.

'Jeremy! You're here already.'

'Your dad and I came back together. Gave us a chance to have a chat, didn't it, old pal?'

Rob had always hated it when Jeremy called him that!

'Yes, well, I'm off to see some mates at The Waterhole. See you later, love. Enjoy yourself.' Then he grasped Jeremy's hand, almost as if he was trying to break it rather than being friendly. 'You take good care of my daughter. You hear me?'

'What's going on?' demanded Gail as soon as the door shut behind him.

'Nothing.' Jeremy topped up his glass and then handed Gail one. 'Your father is just looking out for you like any man would do for his daughter. Maybe one day, I'll do the same for ours.'

'Ours?' Gail felt herself going red. 'Do you mean …?'

'Of course I do.' Jeremy drew her to him.' I'm not going to get down on my knee again. I did all that before and this time, well, it's special. We know what each other is like. We're aware of each other's faults and good points. Gail, will you marry me? Stop! You don't have to say yes or no at this point. I just want you to think about it. But it would be good if you could give me some indication. Like another kiss, maybe?'

Some time later, when Jeremy was in the shower and she was still lying in bed, Gail knew exactly what her answer was going to be. But maybe Jeremy was right, she thought with an air of excitement tingling through her. Perhaps she would wait until later to tell him about her decision. Was she mad? Yes. No. The truth was that there simply wasn't anyone like Jeremy.

And she loved him. She really did.

***

Gail wasn't looking forward to work with Paul on Monday morning. And clearly it showed.

'Gail,' Paul tapped his pen on the desk as though she was a naughty schoolgirl, 'we're meant to be talking business here but I don't believe you've taken in a word I've been saying.'

'You're right.' She pushed away her notepad. 'The fact is that I want to talk about our so-called engagement and when you're going to break the news to Mr Udagawa.'

'Let me worry about that.'

'You haven't told him yet have you?'

'Just leave it, will you?'

'How dare you speak to me like that!'

'Who's the boss here?'

'You're right.' Gail got up. 'Maybe I should tell our client myself. And perhaps I'll tell him at the same time, that I've decided to marry someone else.'

Paul went very still. 'You don't mean … Please don't tell me you're talking about that rat of an ex-husband of yours?' His face darkened. 'Do you really think he loves you? Or is this all about getting the money for Number 13?'

Gail felt a nervous throbbing in her chest.

'In fact,' continued Paul, 'I heard that he's testing that car of his right now. Go on. Take the rest of the day off and go to him. It's worth it to me so you can finally see what a fool you've made of yourself – not to mention the rest of us.'

***

Please! Hurry up! The traffic was terrible. Gail couldn't help honking on the horn even though it wasn't the driver in front who was at fault. In reply he honked back which made her feel even worse.

Love is meant to bring out the best in you. Not the worst. Hadn't that been one of her mum's favourite sayings?

At last! Gail pulled into the car park. Someone else was getting out of his car too. It was her dad!

'What are you doing here?'

'Nice to see you too, Dad.'

'I was going to come and find you actually, after I'd been to the track.'

Something wasn't right. She could feel it.

'What's wrong?'

'Nothing.'

'Is it about Jeremy testing out the car? Paul said he was doing it right now.' She scanned the track, shading her eyes from the sun. 'I can't see anyone.'

He sighed. 'Come and sit next to me in the car for a minute.'

Gail did so, her heart pounding. 'Just tell me.'

'The thing is, you're right. He wants to get her back on the track. "Can't wait any longer …" Those were his exact words.'

He stopped. Why did she feel there was something else?

'And?'

Rob rubbed his face with his hands, leaving a small oil stain on his cheek. Normally Gail would have rubbed it off but this was more important.

Her heart was in her throat. 'Go on, Dad.'

Rob looked away. 'We were at the garage. I heard him on the phone. It sounded like he was telling someone he'd soon be home – and with the car.'

Home?

She opened the car door. 'I want to be sick.'

'I might have been wrong.'

As he spoke, there was the sound of an engine starting. In the distance, she could see a figure approaching another car on the track. It was Number 13.

'The bloody fool.' Rob started to run. 'The parts haven't come in yet. We told him to wait.'

Gail ran behind but Rob was faster. They were arguing loudly.

'I just want to test the steering,' she could hear Jeremy saying.

'Then go slowly. Do you hear me?'

'Jeremy!'

Gail finally caught up just as he was putting on his helmet. 'Tell me the truth. Have you been lying to me again?'

How dare he ignore her? Or was it possible he hadn't heard through his helmet?

Stunned, Gail watched him climb in the car, rev up and zoom off down the track.

'He's going too fast!'

Rob's words sent a chill running through her.

'What on earth is the man doing?'

Gail closed her eyes. 'I can't look, Dad. I just can't. Tell me what's happening. PLEASE.'

Eleven

PAUL

How was he going to get through all this? Paul gazed despairingly at the pile of papers in front of him. Each one demanded his immediate attention. If only he could concentrate. Before Gail came to work for him, he'd have got through this lot in no time. But now all kinds of things were going through his mind ...

Damn. The phone. Not again. He'd had enough interruptions as it was.

'Paul Robinson speaking.'

'Mate, it's Rob. I've ... I've got some bad news.'

Paul's heart quite literally felt as though it was turning over in his chest. Something had happened to Gail! She'd been run over. She was ill. Please let her be all right. He'd give anything – this whole bloody corporation if necessary – for her to be safely in one piece. Or maybe she'd been daft enough to elope with that no-good ex-husband of hers.

'It's Jeremy.' Rob didn't sound himself. 'I'm … I'm afraid he's been killed.'

'Killed?' Paul repeated. A sudden vision of someone plunging a knife into him came to mind. It wouldn't surprise him. That slippery so and so must have enough enemies.

'There was a crash.' Rob had a catch in his voice. 'The stupid bloke wouldn't wait until I got these spare parts. Insisted on driving round the circuit too fast. Then the car … it just came off and smashed into the barrier.'

He could barely talk now and Paul had to strain to hear each word. 'Burst into flames. No one could get near for ages. And the worst of it was that Gail was there …'

'My God. Was she hurt?'

'No. She was watching from the stand.'

'How is she?'

'Numb. I think she's in shock.'

'Can I come round?'

'Maybe in a few hours. Just give her a bit of time.'

Putting down the receiver, Paul sat and stared at the papers in front of him. To think they had seemed important just now. Jeremy was dead. Gail was safe, thank God. But what kind of effect was this going to have on her? And – even though this was selfish to even think about – what kind of effect was it going to have on them?

***

A few hours, Rob had said. But Paul simply couldn't wait that long. He needed to be with Gail at her time of need. That's what friends were for, wasn't it?

Paul knocked again at Number 22. Perhaps she hadn't heard the first time and the bell didn't seem to be working. Footsteps! He held his breath, wondering now if he should have hung on a bit.

'Paul.'

It was Gail herself. Very pale but looking, well, quite normal. 'How are you?'

This was weird. She was talking as if nothing had happened.

'I'm so sorry.' Unable to help himself, Paul pulled her towards him in a hug. Her skin felt so soft. She smelt of that lovely rose perfume she always wore. Then he stepped away. 'How are you doing? I'm sorry, that's a stupid question. Can I do anything to help?'

'No. It's fine. Come in. Please. Would you like a beer? Or a cup of coffee?'

What was going on? Gail was so cool. Had Rob made a mistake? Was Jeremy actually dead?

'You heard what happened then,' Gail said slowly, opening the fridge door for the milk. 'Jeremy was driving too fast. Nothing new there, I suppose. But his luck ran out this time.'

Her voice was flat, almost as if she was telling a story which wasn't really true. She wasn't even crying.

'Look love.' Paul put a hand on her shoulder. 'You're in shock. You need to see Clive. Let me call him for you.'

Gail moved away. 'I don't need a doctor. Listen, I'm going to have a bath. Are you okay to stay with Dad? He's having a bit of a sit down in the lounge room. I think he could do with some company. See you later.'

'Sure.' Feeling really worried now, Paul went through to find Rob. The poor bloke was sitting on the sofa, his head in his hands.

When he heard Paul come in, he looked up briefly and then down again. 'It's my fault. I should never have let Jeremy get in the car. It wasn't ready. But I couldn't stop him. It's as if he was possessed.'

Paul sat down next to him. 'Look, there was nothing you could have done. Like you said, the man knew what he was doing. He always was stubborn.'

'That's as maybe. But what's going to happen now? My daughter's never going to get over this. I know she won't.'

Just what Paul had feared.

'This guilt is going to be with me forever. I'm so tired.' Rob leaned his head back on the sofa. 'Don't be offended, mate, but I could do with some shut eye.'

Paul stood up. He'd outstayed his welcome long enough.

'Look, I'm going to give you guys some time on your own but I'll be back with some food and … and whatever else you need.'

Rob shook his head. 'The only thing we need is for that stupid ex-son-in-law of mine to come walking in here and say he's still alive.'

Paul quietly shut the door behind him and went to Number 26. He needed to tell Gran what had happened – if she hadn't heard already.

To think that only a few hours ago he'd been wishing that Jeremy would get off the scene for ever. But now that he had, life seemed to be even more complicated than ever.

GAIL

'Dad? Please don't cry.' Gail sat down on the sofa next to him, her hair still damp. 'Look, we've got to get on. In fact, I've just been packing up some of Jeremy's things. I've got to get myself organised. I'm working tomorrow and I need to be sorted.'

'Work?' Rob looked up. 'You can't go in. Not when your husband has just died.'

'Ex-husband, Dad. Remember?'

She brought a photograph out of her pocket. 'Look what I found in Jeremy's stuff. One of our wedding pictures. He looks so happy, don't you think? And so do I.'

Rob had stopped crying. He sounded almost angry now. 'Have you forgotten what that man did to you?'

Gail moved away. 'Like I said, I'm really busy now sorting out his stuff.'

Rob's hand caught hers. 'Don't keep things in, love. It's not good for you. Don't you see that?'

'Good for me? Come on, Dad. I never had a chance. If Jeremy had to choose between me and the car, it would be Number 13. Every time.'

He nodded as if relieved. 'That's right, my girl. Let it out. Who's that at the door now?'

It was Jim. Was the whole street going to come and see them?

'Look, sorry to bother you.' He seemed awkward instead of his usual confident self. 'I just wanted to see how you were both doing.'

Rob groaned. 'Bloody awful. It was my fault. I let that stupid idiot drive the car ...'

'No, Dad. Jeremy insisted on getting in. No one could stop him from doing anything he wanted. We both know that. Jeremy bought the car. And it killed him, just like it did his dad. Simple as that.'

Both men were staring at her as if she'd just said something really cruel. Maybe she had. This was all too much. Suddenly the reality was beginning to dawn. Jeremy was never coming back. He had died a horrible death. The flames. The screams …

Gail sank her head into her lap. How was she ever going to cope with this? 'I loved him,' she wept. 'I know he was stupid but I really loved him.'

Rob took her hand, but she shook him off. 'I'm sorry,' she blurted out between sobs. 'I know you mean well. But can you go? Both of you? I just need some time on my own.'

***

That was better. Or was it? The silence helped her to think but at the same time it made her feel so alone. Going back to her room, Gail lay on the bed and reached under her pillow. No one else knew that ever since she and Jeremy had split, she'd found comfort in the small cuddly koala which he'd bought on their honeymoon.

Now, holding it against her skin, she allowed herself to drift back in time. They'd been so happy then. What could she have done to make things different? Jeremy had acted badly. Of course he had. But it always took two …

Not the door again! It couldn't be Dad because he had a key. No doubt it was one of the neighbours, coming round to give more condolences.

'I'm so sorry to bother you,' said the pretty blonde woman on the doorstep.

Did she live on the street? Gail's mind went into a spin. There had been so many comings and goings recently that it was hard to keep track.

'My name is Meredith. Meredith Lord. I'm looking for my husband.'

'Your husband?' Gail repeated disbelievingly.

'Yes. Jeremy. He told me he was staying at Number 22 Ramsay Street.' She looked behind Gail's shoulder as if expecting to see him. 'Is he here right now?'

Part of Gail wanted to cry. The other wanted to laugh. Why wasn't she surprised? It was all beginning to make sense now. Jeremy might be dead. But he had still managed to fool her from the other side of the grave. Only someone as arrogant as Jeremy would have told his wife where he was staying and not worried about being found out. Then she took another look at this woman's kind sweet face. There was a trusting look about this Meredith which reminded Gail of herself when she'd married Jeremy. Maybe, like her, she didn't believe her husband was capable of infidelity. Poor thing. Had Jeremy treated her with the same lack of respect too?

'Come on in,' she said slowly. 'There's something I need to tell you.'

Twelve

GAIL

The door went again just a few minutes after Meredith had left. This time Gail was so relieved to see Paul that she almost threw her arms around his neck. She had to confide in someone.

'I can still hardly believe it.' Her hands shook on the glass of whisky which Paul had pressed into her hand. She never usually drank the stuff but it seemed to help.

'This Meredith woman said she'd flown down from Brisbane to see Jeremy. So I had to tell her that he'd died. It was awful. She burst into floods of tears and I had to comfort her.'

Paul sounded uncertain. 'Did you tell her that he'd proposed even though he was still married?'

'No. I wanted to but there wasn't really the right moment.'

'Where is she now?'

'Gone to sort out a hotel. I couldn't suggest Lassiters. That would be too much. She asked if she could come back later. I couldn't say no.'

Gail put down the glass and began walking up and down the room. 'I'm so stupid. Such a fool. Go on, say it.'

'Say what?'

'You were right all along. You could see what kind of a man he was. He was just using me!'

Paul shrugged. 'But it's not easy getting over an ex, no matter how badly they've behaved. I know that.'

'You do, don't you?' Gail glanced up at Paul gratefully. Then she took the wedding photograph from the mantelpiece where she'd left it from earlier and ripped it into four bits. 'When that woman comes back, I'm going to tell her the truth about her *darling* husband.'

'Are you sure? Don't you think that would be unkind right at this moment?'

'No. I've had to bear the pain. Why shouldn't she?'

'Well you'd better get ready then.' Paul was looking through the window. 'Because it looks as though she's coming up the path. At least, if this is the woman you've been talking about ...'

***

When was she going to leave? All she could talk about was what a great guy Jeremy was while sobbing loudly at the same time. Gail glared at the blonde sitting on her sofa with Paul next to her, offering consolation just as he had done to her earlier. It would be so easy to blow her world apart. Jeremy had done the same to her. So why shouldn't she pass on the favour?

'Actually, Meredith,' said Gail sharply. 'There's

something I need to ask you about your husband.'

Meredith stopped crying and raised her head. Her eyes were bloodshot. She didn't look so attractive now. Paul meanwhile was looking at her with that 'just be careful' expression she'd learned to read so well over the last few weeks.

'You wanted to discuss the funeral service,' said Paul quickly. 'That's what you told me, wasn't it Gail?'

'Right. We wondered if ...'

Meredith cut in. 'Before I can even think about that, I need to know more facts. What I still don't get is why he was staying here with you. He said he was staying with friends.'

Gail twisted the ring on the third finger of her left hand. It had belonged to her mother but she'd put it there after throwing away her wedding ring to ease the emptiness. Meredith saw her action.

'Were you closer to him than he made out?' she asked quietly. The tears had gone now. In their place was fear.

Gail couldn't even look at Paul. There were some things that had to be done, no matter how hard they were. 'It's not that simple,' she began.

Meredith leaned forward. 'Gail. I only took in your surname to begin with. But now I see. You were his ex-wife, weren't you? Of course. I should have guessed. I don't know why I didn't before. But the shock ... I just can't think straight.'

Gail pulled up a chair next to her. 'I get that. In fact, there's more I need to tell you ...'

'Not now,' said Paul quickly. 'I think Meredith needs to rest. Look, I know you went out to find a hotel but I'd like to put you up at Lassiters. I know you'll be comfortable there.'

What was he doing? Whose side was he on?

'That's very kind.' Meredith leaned back against the sofa. 'Jeremy always said that you and he had remained on good terms. That was so like him. He was a good kind man. It's something I'll be sure to tell this little one.'

She stroked her stomach gently.

For the first time, Gail noticed a small rounded bump.

'That's right.' Meredith began to cry again. 'I'm expecting Jeremy's baby. That's why I came – to surprise him with the news. But now that's never going to be possible.'

A baby? Gail felt the shock waves go through her again. Then she couldn't possibly tell this woman the truth. Not now. That really wouldn't be fair.

'I want it to be a boy,' sobbed Meredith. 'And I want him to be just like his father when he grows up.'

'Hah!' This time Gail couldn't contain her feelings any more.

Again, Meredith stopped crying. She could certainly turn those tears on and off. 'Tell me, there wasn't more to Jeremy's feelings for you was there? You know, not many couples stay on "good terms" after a divorce. '

'I don't know,' said Paul quickly.

He was giving her a chance, Gail realised. A way out. If she chose to take it. A few minutes ago, she had been more than happy to give away Jeremy. But a baby changed everything. How ironic that when she'd wanted to start a family with Jeremy, he'd said they weren't 'in a position to do so' yet.

'Actually,' Gail now said, forcing herself to look

Meredith right in the eye, 'Jeremy did nothing but talk about you and how he couldn't wait to get home.'

Then she looked at Paul. 'See,' she tried to say with her face. 'I can be big too.'

His eyes smiled back at her. Then Gail found herself saying something she hadn't intended. 'In fact, why don't you stay here with me instead of at Lassiters or another hotel? It will be much nicer.'

'Really?' All the doubt in Meredith's expression appeared to have melted away.

'Absolutely. Now how about another cup of tea?'

'Thank you. Can I have two sugars? I never used to have it sweet but my taste buds seem to have changed since I found I was expecting this little one.'

And that's exactly why I'm being so nice, Gail told herself as she went out into the kitchen. Hurting Jeremy and his wife was one thing. But she couldn't bring herself to hurt a little baby. One day that child would grow up. And it was important that he or she didn't know the truth about that no-good father.

'Damn you, Jeremy,' she muttered. 'Damn you.'

***

It turned out that Meredith wanted Jeremy's funeral to be held in Brisbane where they had both lived together as man and wife – a 'small' detail which Jeremy had failed to mention when he'd been trying to get Gail back just before his death. 'You're very welcome to come to the service,' Meredith said when she was preparing to leave. Paul happened to be there at the time for support; something which Gail was grateful for.

The last few days had been difficult, with Gail trying to

be kind to the poor woman, while at the same time being furious about Jeremy's deceit. On many occasions she'd been tempted to tell Meredith the truth. But what good would that do?

'I think it's best that I don't,' said Gail in reply, touching her arm.

The other woman hugged her. 'You've been so kind to me. Thank you.'

Gail swallowed hard as she forced herself to look at Meredith's swollen stomach. If Jeremy had behaved himself, then they might have had a baby together. 'Good luck with the pregnancy. Let me know when it's born, won't you?'

'I will.'

Together she and Paul stood at the window, watching Meredith get into the taxi. 'You did very well,' he said quietly.

'I tried.' Gail turned, wiping her eyes. 'Just as you did.'

He stiffened. 'What do you mean?'

'Come on, Paul. We've spent all this time together in the last few months, both as colleagues and good friends, but there's a lot we just ignore or skate over, isn't there?'

She blew her nose. 'I'm not just talking about Jeremy. I'm talking about Terry too.'

He moved away from her. 'There's a reason for that. It's in the past.'

Gail caught his hand and led him to the sofa close by. 'But it's still haunting you. I can see it in your eyes. I've heard snatches of gossip but I don't really know the truth. Won't you tell me? We know each other well enough now.'

Paul sighed. 'You're a strong-minded woman, Gail.

Like she was.'

Gail waited.

'If you really want to know, Terry had a criminal past. In fact, she'd been married to a bank robber before we met.'

Gail let out a small gasp. Somehow she couldn't imagine Paul being involved with anyone like that!

Paul noted her expression. 'I was pretty shocked when the truth came out but ... well, we were in love.' He spread out his hands. 'What can I say?'

'I understand,' said Gail quietly. 'I did some crazy things in the name of love too. But what happened then?'

Paul looked down at the ground as if scared of meeting her eyes. 'A man called Charles Durham, who knew her first husband, started threatening her. Terry was scared it was going to ruin her new life with me so ... well, she shot him dead.'

Gail could barely speak. This was far worse than she'd realised.

'When I found out what she'd done,' continued Paul in a low voice, 'I said I was going to the police.'

Gail nodded. 'Of course. You had to. It was the right thing.'

'Terry didn't think so. She begged me not to and when I wouldn't listen, she shot me too.'

'What?'

Aghast, she watched as Paul pulled up his shirt to reveal a scar on his shoulder. 'I survived but she went to prison for murdering Charles Durham and for assaulting me.' His face darkened. 'And if that wasn't bad enough, she wrote to me, asking me to visit. But I was mad with her and revolted by what she'd done. I mean … murder!'

He raised his head and Gail could see that his eyes were red with pain and anger and hurt. His voice rang out like an animal in pain. 'So she killed herself.'

Gail put her hands to her mouth. 'I'm so sorry.'

He jumped to his feet. 'Now you can see why I can never forgive myself and why I'm scared about committing myself to another relationship. If I'd gone to visit her behind bars, my wife might never have killed herself. I might as well be guilty of killing her myself.'

'No, of course you're not. That's silly.'

Gail stood up now, trying to hold his hand in comfort but he pulled it away. 'I never want to be hurt by love again,' he groaned.

'That's exactly how I feel,' murmured Gail.

Still. At least they'd cleared the air. And, just as important, she knew what she was going to do next.

PAUL

'Are you certain?'

Gail and he were sitting on the patio. The light had almost faded now but she'd switched on the outside lights.

'Perfectly sure. Just draw up the contract.'

Paul couldn't help feeling uneasy. 'You won't change your mind again?'

'No. You were right. Marrying for love was a mistake I won't make twice.'

How romantic! He made a noise that was a sort of half-laugh.

'This is a business arrangement. Right?' she said.

Paul forced himself to sound more certain than he

really felt. 'Absolutely.'

'As long as we're clear about that.'

His mind shifted into practical mode. 'We'll need to sort out a lot of stuff like bank accounts.'

'Separate, of course,' Gail said quickly.

'Absolutely.'

'I don't want a church service.'

'I get that.' He brought out his diary. 'How about four weeks from tomorrow?'

'Great.'

They could have been scheduling a work meeting. Yet wasn't that exactly what this marriage was about?

'Mr Udagawa will be pleased.'

Now it was her turn to make a noise. 'That's why we're doing this. Right?'

'And for security,' he added.

'Sure.'

There was a noise as the patio doors slid open.

'Dad,' said Gail.

Rob sat down heavily. 'That man had us all fooled, didn't he? I could wring his neck if he was still alive. Coming here to get money out of us for his car and making eyes at my daughter when he had a wife all the time ... And I don't get how you could have had her under this roof ...'

'Because it felt the right thing to do.'

'I'm really proud of Gail,' said Paul. 'She could have said a lot but she didn't. And I'm proud of her for another reason too. Your daughter has just agreed the date to become my wife.'

'Really?' Rob's eyes lit up. 'That's great news, mate. I'm really pleased.' Then he pumped his hand.

'Congratulations.'

'Thanks. I can hardly believe my luck.'

It was true, Paul told himself as he made his way home. Of course Gail had only changed her mind because of the shock over Jeremy. But you never knew. Maybe she might learn to care for him. And if she didn't? Well, enough marriages had been made for convenience over the years. It wasn't as though conventional love had worked for either of them before. Maybe this was the way forward after all. As long as she went through with it.

***

GAIL

'Are you sure, love?' Rob asked after Paul had gone.

'Quite sure.' Gail busied herself tidying up the lounge room. 'I couldn't let Meredith know the truth. It wouldn't be fair on the baby.'

'I'm not talking about Meredith. I'm talking about this marriage of yours to Paul.'

She turned her back so he wouldn't see her face. 'I'm sure about that too.'

'Okay then.' He didn't sound convinced. But it wasn't any of his business.

'I'm off to turn in now.'

'See you tomorrow, Dad.'

Gail waited until his door had shut. Then she went to the bin and pulled out the torn photograph pieces. 'I used to love you so much,' she told Jeremy's smiling face. 'But now I'm going to be practical.' Then, without knowing why, she held the shredded picture tenderly against her cheek for a brief second before putting it back in the bin.

Thirteen

PAUL

'I've told you before. I don't like my eggs like that.'

'Too bad, son. It's the way I do them. I've been making eggs for years. If you're not happy, wait till I've finished and you can do your own.'

Scott slammed down his fork. 'Don't worry. I will.'

Teenagers!

Paul raised his eyebrows at Gail as they walked in through the door to catch the usual breakfast argument between Jim and Scott. 'Hope you're ready for this,' he whispered.

She nodded. But inside, Paul's heart was beating. He wasn't just referring to the domestic chaos of Number 26. That was nothing compared with the big step they were about to take.

'How lovely to see you both!' Helen looked up from the newspaper. Great, thought Paul, as he took in the headline.

RACING CAR STAR KILLED IN HORRIFIC CRASH, LEAVING NEW WIFE TO GRIEVE

'I hadn't realised Jeremy was married,' Helen said. There was an edge to her voice which suggested disapproval – as though she had been deliberately kept in the dark.

'I hadn't known either, Helen,' said Gail crisply. 'Not until he'd died, anyway. Apparently she's expecting his baby. It can't be easy for her.'

Then she linked her arm into Paul's. He patted it reassuringly. Either Gail was a very good actress or else Jeremy's final betrayal had finally made her see what a rat he was. Paul only hoped it was the latter.

'I see.' Helen glanced back at the headline and then folded the paper, placing it by the side of her plate. 'Would you like anything to eat? You need to keep your strength up with everything going on.'

Instinctively, Paul sensed his gran wasn't comfortable.

'We've set a date,' he chipped in. 'We're getting married in four weeks.'

'Really?' said Jim, who'd handed over the pan to Scott and had now joined them at the table with his sunny-side up fried eggs.

'Quite soon, then.' Helen was giving them both a look which could mean almost anything. Sometimes Paul thought he could read Gran's mind and sometimes he didn't have a clue about what was going on inside. Like now.

Then suddenly, she clapped her hands. 'We must have an engagement party then! What do you think, Jim?'

'Sure. If that's what the young couple want.'

Gail laughed. 'Not so young now but thanks anyway.'

'Not so old either,' Paul added. 'You can fall in love whatever your age.'

'Just listen to him!' Scott gave a playful 'air' punch. 'Got it bad, haven't you, mate?'

Gail was flushing. 'Actually Helen, if it's all the same to you, I think we'll skip an engagement party. We're past that kind of thing.'

'Really?' Helen put her head to one side as if considering this. 'That's a shame.' She got up from her chair. 'Now if you'll excuse me, I've got some errands to sort out.'

'And we've got to be off too.' Paul had his hand on Gail's shoulder. 'We've got some very important shopping to do.'

'We have?'

'Just wait and see.'

'That's the spirit,' said Jim, who didn't seem to realise that there was yolk dribbling down his mouth. 'Make sure you know who's boss from the start!'

***

It was a beautiful day. Everyone they passed on the street into town seemed to be a couple. It felt pretty good, Paul told himself, to be one too. Especially when you had a beautiful, intelligent woman like Gail walking next to you. There were times, however, when he found himself wishing this was for real …

'So what's this shopping you've got to do?' asked Gail.

'*We've* got to do,' corrected Paul. He stopped outside the jeweller's. 'I thought we could choose an engagement ring. I mean, you could choose one. Any one you fancy.'

Gail sighed. 'Honestly, Paul. I don't really feel in the mood.'

Suddenly he felt horribly deflated. 'Look, I know the last few weeks have been tough. But we've got to have one to keep up the …' His voice tailed off, not wanting to say the word.

'Act?' suggested Gail.

He nodded. 'Gran was suspicious. I could just tell. But if you have a ring, she might be more convinced.'

Gail shrugged. 'If that's what you want.'

'How about that one?' Paul pointed out a beautiful sapphire.

'Are you kidding? That's just like the one Jeremy gave me.'

'I didn't know.'

'I used to wear it when I was working. You don't remember?'

'No. Sorry.'

She gave a little sigh. 'No reason why you should. I'm just being silly. What about that diamond over there?'

Paul felt a shiver go through him. 'Actually, that's quite like the one I gave my wife.'

Gail shook her head. 'We're a right pair, aren't we?'

'That ruby looks lovely.'

Gail nodded. 'It'll do. Red seems appropriate, doesn't it?'

'Why?'

'Because it seems to me that an arranged marriage is a bit like playing with fire. It could warm you. Or it could burn you.' Then she withdrew her arm from Paul's and walked through the shop door, leaving him to follow.

***

'So we thought,' said Paul the next evening, 'that we'd do a swap. You could move into my room at Lassiters and I …'

'… will take my place at Number 22.' Rob finished the sentence for him. 'Great idea. Wouldn't do to have the father-in-law living with the happy couple, would it?'

Gail looked worried. 'Sure you don't mind, Dad? I don't want you being lonely.'

'No chance of that in a hotel like Lassiters.' He winked. 'I'll have a ball of a time. Don't you worry about me. Like the ring, by the way. And I'm really glad you're having an engagement party after all.'

'Gran said we'd regret it if we didn't.' Paul glanced at Gail who had gone rather quiet. 'She said it would mark a fresh start for both of us.'

'Certainly will!' Rob was beaming from ear to ear. 'I know we haven't always seen eye to eye, lad. But I can tell you one thing. I know my daughter will be in safe hands with you. Not like that ex-husband …'

'Sorry.' Gail was getting to her feet. 'I just need to powder my nose.'

'Sure, love.'

Paul watched her walk away with a sinking feeling in his chest.

'Did I just say something?' asked Rob.

'Maybe,' said Paul, 'it might be best if we didn't talk too much about Jeremy.'

'Suits me. Never did care for the man. Dishonest. That's what he was.' He grasped Paul's hand in a man-shake. 'The great thing about you, is that I know you're straight-talking, through and through. You wouldn't hide anything from anyone. I can rest assured that my daughter is in safe hands with you. And that's all that any father could want.'

***

At Gail's request, they kept the number of guests to a minimum. Just a few friends from Ramsay Street and, of course, Mr Udagawa who kept beaming all the way through. 'I am so honoured you invite me here,' he said again and again to anyone who would listen. 'Family is very important to me. I like my business associates to have the same values.'

Gail looked beautiful in that powder-blue dress which went so well with her light-brown hair. Paul kept looking at her, unable to believe that she was really his. Even though she wasn't. How could he have misjudged her at the airline? Or was it that he had changed? Maybe both of them had. Certainly in those days, neither of them would have considered an arranged marriage. Rob's comments about him being honest, through and through, still made him feel uneasy. If only he knew the truth.

He was also worried that Gail was having second thoughts. She was very quiet at the party. 'Speech, speech,' someone called out after Paul had delivered a few brief words about how lucky he was. But Gail had shaken her head and said that Paul had said all there was to say and that she couldn't add any more.

The following day was an office day. The start of a busy week ahead.

'Have you got a second?' said Gail coming in. Wow! Every time he looked at her, she seemed more gorgeous.

'For my beautiful fiancée?' He stood up. 'Of course.'

Gail shut the door quickly. 'Quit the act. Please.'

Paul felt that fluttering of unease again.

'Look,' she said, sitting down opposite him. 'The party got me thinking. I can't go through with this, Paul. I really can't. It's a sham. I had enough of that with Jeremy.'

Paul got up and came round to the other side of the desk. 'But you promised. And remember that we're just doing this for business – as well as to stop us getting hurt again. Life isn't easy, is it?'

She shook her head.

Encouraged, he went on. 'It's nicer having someone there to help you – especially when you've known each other a long time like we have. There are no surprises. We don't expect anything apart from companionship. More people should follow our example! It's just a fairy tale that a couple have to be madly in love to get married. I reckon there would be far fewer divorces if everyone else was as practical and realistic as us.'

To his huge relief, Gail nodded. 'Maybe you're right. When you put it like that, I feel much better. It was just the party and, well, this.' She stretched out her left hand. The ruby gleamed in the sunlight streaming through the window. 'It's such a commitment.'

'If it doesn't work,' Paul said gently, 'we can always get divorced.'

She shuddered. 'I wouldn't want to go through that again.'

'But it would be different if there isn't love involved.'

Was he kidding himself?

'Sure. Okay.'

Phew!

'Aren't you going to answer that?' She indicated the phone. 'It's been ringing for ages.'

Had it? Paul had been so desperate to change Gail's mind that he hadn't noticed.

'Dad. Hi. What? Well that's great news, isn't it? I see. Well, I get your point but … Yes. I'll tell her. Look, I'll come round later.'

Gail was staring at him expectantly. 'What's going on?'

'Scott and Charlene are getting married too! Imagine that?'

'They seem very young,' said Gail slowly.

'Exactly! They're actually under-age at the moment!'

'But they've been together for a while.'

'That's not the point. The two of them are virtually children. How can they make a big decision like this? They'll be divorced before they're thirty – if not before.'

'You're such a sceptic. Some childhood romances do last, you know.' She was looking rather wistful. 'I actually think it's sweet. At least one couple in the family is tying the knot for the right reasons.'

'I thought we'd sorted that out.'

'We have. Sorry.' Then she brought some papers out of her bag. 'Have you got a minute? I just need you to go through these ideas for the restaurant.'

'Sure. But you will come back to Number 26 with me after work, won't you?' Paul's jaw set as he spoke. 'I suppose we'll need to congratulate Scott and Charlene.' He shook his head. 'I can't believe my brother is so stupid. He's virtually a schoolkid.'

Gail touched his arm briefly. 'I can see why you're

worried. To be honest, so am I. But if they're set on it, who are we to stop them?'

***

'So,' joked Paul, 'you had to copy your big brother, Scott!'

'Paul!' squealed Lucy, rushing over to him for a hug.

'Where's Dad?'

'Out in the backyard sorting out the barbecue.'

Jim's face was black – and not just from the charcoal. 'Those kids are far too young to get married,' he grumbled. 'He'll change. So will Charlene. Then they'll find they're not suited any more. They need time to grow as their own people. You just mark my words. I've told him so but he won't listen and now he's hardly talking to me.'

'I'm not surprised.' Paul took the fork and turned over the steaks, which were getting burned. 'Kids don't like to be told what to do. Maybe they need to make their own mistakes. Or maybe it will work out after all.'

'Well at least one of you kids is being sensible.'

Yeah, right!

'Jim,' called out Helen. 'Come and help me with the rubbish, will you? And Paul, you're neglecting your fiancée. She wants a word.'

Gail was already wandering out into the backyard. 'Everything all right?' asked Paul nervously. Please don't let her have changed her mind again.

'Yes. Apart from one thing.'

He knew it!

'I think we should put Scott and Charlene's wedding before our own.' She lowered her voice. 'After all, their marriage will be for real. Not like ours.'

Paul's heart sang with relief. So she wasn't trying to bow out again. 'Whatever you want.'

'Our wedding needs to be really small so we don't overshadow it.'

'Actually,' said Paul slowly, 'what do you think if we …'

***

A week later

'You look beautiful.'

It was true. Paul could barely take his eyes off Gail. That little cream suit was stunning. So elegant and yet at the same time contemporary. She could be a film star. It took him back to the days when at least one of the passengers on a flight would try and ask her out on a date.

'You look good yourself,' she said. Then she stood on tiptoes. 'Just let me straighten that tie of yours.'

'What do you think of all this?' He gestured to the vases which were overflowing with flowers and to the buckets of champagne on ice. The lounge room almost looked like a superior hotel suite.

'You did a great job.'

They'd agreed that Paul should be in charge of the details. Gail had said she was 'too busy'.

'Are you still sure?' she asked.

'Absolutely. You?'

Before she could answer, the door opened. 'Dad!' Paul watched as she hugged Rob.

'This is some do!' Rob was looking around, astounded. 'What's going on?'

Gail flushed. 'What do you mean? It's just a bit of a gathering.'

'You can say that again. Champagne? Flowers? And look at the two of you, all dressed up.'

'Paul! Gail!'

Just in time. His lot were arriving now. And their other guest.

Paul clicked his glass with a spoon. 'Welcome everyone. Thanks for coming. Before I go any further, I'd like to introduce you to Mr Downley.'

The man in the grey suit gave a half wave.

'Mr Downley is a wedding registrar.' Paul paused, his heart beating. 'He's here to witness a wedding. That's right. This isn't just another family party. It's the occasion of our wedding. And this, of course, is my beautiful bride.'

He put out his hand to Gail who came to stand shyly by his side. Her hand felt as nervous and clammy as his own.

'I knew something was going on,' boomed Rob.

'How romantic!' Helen clapped her hands. 'I've never been to a surprise wedding before.'

There was a murmur around of 'You're kidding me' and 'That was quick, wasn't it?'

'Shall we start the ceremony?' said Mr Downley.

Paul felt as though he was in a trance. It didn't seem any time at all until he and Gail were pronounced man and wife.

'You may kiss the bride,' said Mr Downley.

Tentatively, he gave her a little peck on her cheek.

'Call that a kiss!' yelled Rob.

Scott thumped the ground in agreement. 'Come on

Paul, you can do better than that!'

Gail seemed as embarrassed as he was. 'Better get on with it,' her eyes seemed to say. So he did. Her mouth was so soft. And, despite everything, she seemed to be responding more than her earlier apprehension had indicated. Wow! It was just as if he'd discovered kissing for the very first time – a bit like a teenager.

Finally, amidst the cat calls, they broke away. Gail reached up to wipe the lipstick from his mouth. They smiled at each other, knowingly.

'That's it, you two!' called out Scott as Charlene hung onto his arm. 'You're going to have to wait until we've gone now.'

Paul felt a thud of apprehension. What exactly would happen then?

***

'How do you think it went?' asked Gail, collecting the last of the glasses to take into the kitchen.

The guests had all gone now, including Rob who had moved into the hotel.

'Great, I think. I know Dad would've liked us to have a big wedding, but at least it saved your dad having to splash out!'

'That's certainly how he saw it!'

How awkward this was. That wonderful kiss earlier on had now been replaced by nervousness – at least on his part.

He nodded towards the champagne bottle. 'Want any more?'

'No thanks.' She yawned. 'To be honest, I'm exhausted.'

'Let me take that glass off you. I'll finish off the rest.'

'Thanks. Think I'll head off for bed now.'

For a minute, Paul thought she was going to kiss him on the cheek. Then she seemed to change her mind. 'See you in the morning then.'

Paul waited until he heard her footsteps go up the stairs and then the door closing behind her. What would he give to go in after her? But that wasn't what they'd agreed. The spare bed was all made up for him.

Slowly, he took the flower from his suit and placed it in Gail's empty champagne glass. This was certainly very different from his first wedding night. And he wouldn't mind betting it was different from Gail's too.

Despite everything he'd told her, all kinds of doubts were now crowding his mind. This might only be a marriage of convenience but had they done this too soon for it to work? Paul couldn't help thinking that his bride still wasn't over Jeremy. Still, he'd find out. Sooner or later.

Fourteen

GAIL

So here she was! A newly-married woman. It didn't feel real. And, of course, Gail told herself, that's because it wasn't. Ever since the wedding a few days ago, she'd woken up with the same thought. Had she gone mad? What on earth had persuaded her to marry Paul when Jeremy was only just cold in the ground? Then again, hadn't the same Jeremy got a wife that he hadn't mentioned – now a widow – and a baby on the way. What a mess! Was it any wonder that she'd acted on the rebound?

Yet at the same time, there was a strange comfort in knowing that a wedding ring was on her finger. Paul was a good man. Not nearly as arrogant as she'd thought during their airline days. She could do far worse …

He was also a real family man. Wasn't he out now, playing a game of squash with his dad? Not all men would do that, especially when they'd recently got married. He understood too how she felt about her own dad, who could be infuriating at times. But he was still her father and well, family was family. Jeremy could have done with some of that loyalty.

Wandering out into the kitchen – still in her dressing gown – to make a cup of coffee, she spotted a note in Paul's handwriting.

Bad news! Cousin Hilary is coming for Scott and Charlene's wedding. She's a real busybody. We need to be careful!

Actually, this could be quite exciting. Gail had been hearing a lot about this cousin. Apparently she was furious not to be invited to their wedding, even though it had been explained to her that it had been held at short notice. Still, it would be interesting to meet her. Then she tore up the note into little pieces. They certainly couldn't risk anyone else seeing it!

***

When Gail got into the office the next day, the first thing she saw on her desk was a massive bouquet of flowers. 'They've just arrived,' gushed Jane. 'Aren't they gorgeous?'

But it was the name on the card which Gail's eye was drawn to.

Mrs Robinson

How strange and unfamiliar that looked. As though she was another person altogether. For a minute Gail's heart lurched, remembering how excited she'd been when Jeremy had made her 'Mrs Lord'. Now someone else was bearing his name. A woman whom Jeremy had chosen to keep quiet when he'd been trying to persuade her to start again just before his death …

'Got another admirer already?' joked Paul who was close behind her.

Gail flushed. 'I don't know. Let's look at the card.'

She handed it to Paul who groaned. 'Cousin Hilary. Listen to the message. "Thought I'd send you these in place of the wedding present which I would have given you if I'd been present on the day".'

Paul looked embarrassed. 'There's something else. Dad's just told me that she's arrived already.'

'But that's two days early!' gasped Gail.

'I know. She does this sometimes if it's more convenient for her. Gran wondered if we could put her up. Frankly, I'd rather we booked her into the hotel but …'

'Nonsense.' Gail patted him on the arm, aware that Jane was still there, listening to every word. 'She's family. We must make her feel welcome.'

Paul's face was a picture. 'Just be careful.'

She could read him like a book. Of course she would! But it would be interesting to meet Hilary and besides, it might be easier to have a third person around rather than the two of them. After all, it wasn't as though they were a traditional newly-married couple, was it?

***

Was it lunchtime already? The one thing about her new job, thought Gail, was that it kept her on her toes. There was never a boring moment. Still, now was as good a time as any to get a sandwich. No – maybe a salad. Perhaps Dad might like one too. One of the girls at the hotel had mentioned that her father wasn't 'a great one for breakfast'.

'Actually, he normally never misses it,' she'd replied.

'Really?' the girl had said. 'He hasn't been down for any since he arrived. And he hasn't had room service either.'

Gail had meant to check up on this before but so much had been going on.

'Hi, Dad. It's me,' she said into the phone. 'Would you like some lunch?'

There was a silence at the other end as well as a rustling before he spoke. 'No thanks. In a bit of a rush.'

Odd. Dad didn't sound like himself.

'Are you okay?'

'Who?'

'You?'

'Yes. Sure. Why wouldn't I be?'

'Only wondered, as the hotel staff told me you'd been skipping breakfast.'

'They've got no right. Nor you. I'm a grown man. I can do what I please. And I'll thank you not to keep tabs on me.'

Wow. She'd hit a nerve there!

'You're my only dad. Aren't I allowed to do that?'

His voice softened. 'Sorry. It's just that I'm really busy at the garage. There isn't time to eat let alone think.'

Gail felt a flash of guilt. Had she been selfish in encouraging Dad to leave Number 22 so she and Paul could start their 'married life' together? Maybe they should have found a bigger place where they could all have lived.

'Look, Dad. I get that. But I miss you.'

'Miss you too, love.'

That was more like her old dad!

'Come round for dinner tonight. Okay? Cousin Hilary's coming – she's the one they've all been talking about. It would be great if you and Paul could both talk to her while I get on with the cooking.'

'I'm not sure.'

'Dad! Please. For me.'

'Okay. See you there.'

Something didn't sound quite right. Still, Gail told herself, maybe she'd find out tonight.

***

'Would you like some more risotto?' asked Gail.

Hilary had announced, when she arrived, that she was on a 'seafood and rice' diet and that nothing else would do. This had caused a certain amount of consternation but luckily Gail had had some prawns in the fridge and there was just enough rice in the cupboard to go round. The roast chicken which she'd cooked earlier for their guest would keep until tomorrow.

'More?' Hilary raised her eyebrows. 'Not for me, thank you. You're clearly one of those cooks who's liberal with the salt. What kind of rice did you use?'

'Long-grained.'

'Ah.'

She might as well have said, 'So that explains it'.

Their guest looked a bit like an old-fashioned uptight spinster with that severe scraped back hairstyle. However, cousin Hilary had great posture and she really wasn't unattractive. In fact, Gail was dying to take her in hand and give her a makeover. Mind you, she had a feeling that Hilary would take that as an insult – even though the woman was happy to heap out insults to everyone else, including Gail and her cooking!

She offered the dish to everyone else and then took another spoonful herself. No need to let all this go to waste.

'And I'd advise you,' continued Hilary, her eyes fixed on her, 'not to have any more either.' Had she just heard her right? 'If you're pregnant – which I presume you must be – you need to watch your weight. Otherwise you'll have trouble shifting it later on.'

'But I'm not pregnant!'

Hilary gave her a 'come on' look. 'Then why did you get married so fast without asking the whole family?'

By the 'whole family', it was clear that she meant her!

'We didn't want to hang about,' said Paul firmly, placing his hand over hers protectively. Gail felt a flush of gratitude that he'd got her out of a sticky situation.

'Well don't leave it too late.'

'I completely agree,' chipped in Rob. 'Not as though either of you are getting any younger. And I wouldn't mind being a granddad.'

It was the most animated she'd seen him look all evening.

Gail stood up to clear away the plates. This was becoming far more awkward than she'd anticipated.

'I'll help,' said Paul quickly.

Their hands brushed. Embarrassed, Gail moved back. 'It's okay. I can manage.'

'In my opinion, a wife should always make a husband share the chores.' Hilary's eyes were fixed on the hand which Gail had just moved away from Paul's. 'You need to start as you mean to go on.'

'Really? How many times did you say you'd been married?'

Hilary glared at Rob. So did Gail. How dare Dad be so rude to their guest?

'I'm too sensible. That's why I stick to advising others.'

'You might have a point there,' said Gail tartly.

Hilary gave a satisfied nod. 'I should say so. Is that wine bottle just for your side of the table?' She looked meaningfully at her empty glass.

'Let me help you.' This was Paul.

'Thank you. What pretty table mats, by the way. I like the rustic look although personally I always throw mine away if they are a little worn. Clearly you didn't get any as wedding presents.'

Paul rolled his eyes but Gail had gone back to being amused by this forthright woman. At least you knew where you were with her. Which was more, right now, than she could say about Paul and herself.

'Time for bed, I reckon,' said Rob shortly after the meal.

'Really? So soon?'

Rob was normally a night owl.

'I've got a lot to be getting on with so might be wise to set some extra shut eye.'

Something really wasn't right. She just knew it. But what?

***

It had taken a while for her and Paul to clear up. Hilary would have gone to bed by now. 'I think she's really quite nice,' whispered Gail as they tiptoed up the stairs.

'Eccentric nice but quite good fun.'

'Hah. You don't know her. What about that sculpture?' Paul snorted, nudging her. He pointed to the horrendous ornament Hilary had handed to them as a late wedding present. 'It's hideous, isn't it?'

'I've honestly never seen anything like it before. Where on earth do you think she got it?'

'Some bargain basement, I expect.'

They were each standing at the doors of their separate bedrooms now. 'Goodnight then,' he started to say – and then the bathroom door opened.

Hilary! Swiftly, Paul nipped across to Gail's side. 'Thought you'd be asleep by now.'

'I like a long bath. You don't have much water, do you? Need a bigger immersion if you ask me. See you in the morning then. I generally like my tea at seven a.m. With a little bit of honey in it, if you don't mind.'

At last! Cousin Hilary's door was shut now. 'Quick,' giggled Gail.

Paul darted back to his room and gave her a little wave. 'Sure you don't want to try and get pregnant?'

'Very funny,' giggled Gail.

Then she shut the door behind her. But when she was on her own, she couldn't help thinking about Jeremy and his unborn child. When they'd been together, she'd wanted a family but he hadn't been 'ready'. It was all so unfair …

***

In the morning, Gail lay in bed having a quiet chuckle over the events of the previous evening. It had been like one of those comedies with everyone going in and out of doors! Talking of which, there was a knock! Getting out of bed, she could hear Paul and cousin Hilary nattering away outside.

'Hi,' she said opening the door.

Both turned round to face her as though she'd just said something really weird.

'I was explaining to Hilary that we spilt some coffee in our bedroom so we both had to sleep in the spare room.' He emphasised the 'both' while his eyes sent warning signals. Clearly she'd put her foot in it by coming out and showing they hadn't shared the same room.

There was only one thing for it.

'Come on, Paul,' she said. 'I think it's time to tell our guest the truth, don't you? She is family, after all.'

'Are you mad?' said Paul's face.

Hilary's eyes were out on stalks.

Gail was almost enjoying this. 'The thing is that after dinner, Paul and I had an argument.'

Her husband's face cleared. 'Yes. Yes – we did. And you know what, Gail? I still think I'm right. Your father has no right to go on about us having children.'

'You're entitled to your views,' declared Hilary, who was still in her dressing gown. 'However, we can't have any family rows before the wedding. So you, Paul, are going to have to get used to your father-in-law just as he will have to get used to you.'

'Actually, I ...'

'No.' She was wagging a finger. 'That's enough now. If you don't mind, I'm off to the dry cleaners.' She sniffed. 'That shirt of yours smells a bit, Paul. Would you like me to take some of your clothes too?'

'It's my new cologne, actually. Very popular at the moment.'

'Really? Goodness, I'm surprised. Still, no accounting for taste. Now I don't need a key, do I? I expect you'll be in.'

'I was thinking of going out but ...'

'You'll stay in for me. ' She nodded at her own completed sentence. 'Not sure when I'll be back but do remember about my diet, won't you? I wouldn't want to embarrass you by not being able to eat lunch.'

***

What a lovely wedding! As Scott and Charlene made their vows, their faces shining with excitement, Gail felt a lump in her throat. Everyone agreed that Scott and Charlene made a lovely couple. They had everything that she and Paul didn't, Gail reminded herself. Love, truth and honesty. This was the real thing. So different from the business arrangement which she and Paul had agreed on.

The service was really beautiful. The music seemed to be lifting everyone else's spirits apart from her own. All around her were rows of misty-eyed guests, remembering perhaps their own youth when they'd been in love too. Just as she had once been with Jeremy ...

'Now you may kiss the bride!'

Everyone broke out in loud applause. But Gail almost forgot to join in. She'd been too busy searching the faces for Dad. Where was he? It wasn't like him to miss a good wedding. And now here they were, about to go back to Number 26 for the reception and he still hadn't turned up.

'Sorry, Paul, but I'll have to see you later.'

He looked alarmed. 'Why? Where are you going?'

'To find Dad. Something's up. I can feel it.'

'You're not the only one to think so.' Paul glanced worriedly at Hilary who was advancing towards them. 'I think she's on to us.'

'Coo-eee!'

She needed to go. Now. 'I can't help that. I'm more worried about Dad. I need to find out where he is. I'll be back as soon as I can.'

***

The garage was all locked up. If he wasn't in the hotel, Gail told herself, racing towards Lassiters, she didn't know where he was.

But the receptionist, handing her the spare key, informed her that yes, her father had indeed gone up to the room some hours ago.

Some hours ago? Gail felt a qualm going through her. Was he ill?

What a mess! Opening the door, Gail took a step backwards at the scene in front of her. Cans of beer lying everywhere. Bottles too. An overwhelming stink of alcohol and – unless she was mistaken – vomit from the direction of the bathroom.

'Who's there?' slurred the heap on the bed.

Never before had she seen him like this!

'Dad. What's wrong?' He was lying on top of the covers, fully clothed. 'Are you ill?'

'Leave me alone.'

How could he talk to her like that?

'Why did you miss the wedding?'

'I shdidn't feel like it.'

141

'You're plastered!'

'Sho what? That'sh my business.' He raised himself on one elbow and then fell down on the bed again. 'If you must know, I was drinking with my mates and came back for shome few beers on my own.'

Maybe some air might help. Gail went over to the window to open the curtains.

There was a groan from the bed.

'Get rid of that light. It'sh hurting my head.'

'I think something's going on,' said Gail slowly.

'Who ashked you to judge my life. Just get out. Now. Do you hear me?'

Gail was beginning to feel angry now. Maybe there wasn't anything wrong and he had just got plastered after all.

'Fine. I'll leave you to it.'

***

'That's really strange,' said Paul when she went back to the wedding reception and told him what had happened.

The music and lively chatter were so loud that no one else could hear. Or so she'd thought.

'What's really strange?' repeated Hilary coming up to them.

Was that woman following her? Their guest was beginning to be less amusing and more of a nuisance. 'Actually, Hilary, it's a private matter.'

Her eyes narrowed. 'I see. I just hope that you two haven't been having any more rows again. When I initially advised you to start as you mean to go on, this isn't what I meant. By the way, where's that charming father of yours? I was hoping to continue our stimulating conversation.'

'He's been held up,' stepped in Paul smoothly. 'I'm sure he'll be here soon.'

But privately, Gail wasn't so sure.

***

'Best let your dad sleep it off.' That's what Paul had suggested last night when the happy couple had finally left – so sweet! – and he still hadn't turned up.

Gail only hoped he was right. As soon as she woke, she got into the shower – remembering how her first husband sometimes used to come in with her – and dressed. What a beautiful day! If only her own spirits felt a bit brighter. But inside was a niggling feeling that wouldn't go away. A bit like when Jeremy got into that car.

'And where are you off to at this early hour?'

Great! Just when she'd needed time to think. But Hilary was already making coffee in the kitchen as if this was her own home. She'd even re-washed the mugs which had been in the cupboard.

'To see my dad.' She grabbed her keys from the hook. 'Can you tell Paul, I'll be back later.'

'Can't you tell him yourself?' Hilary shook her head. 'Please don't tell me that you two newly-weds are in separate bedrooms again …'

Gail didn't hang around to hear the rest of the sentence. In fact, she couldn't get out of the front door fast enough. Whoops!

Oh dear. She'd collided with a portly gentleman with glasses, a very conventional brown checked-jacket, and a slightly pompous air which inferred he was better than anyone else around him.

'Harold! Sorry.'

'Gail.' He frowned, creating a deep line between his eyes. 'Have you seen your father?'

'I think he's at Lassiters,' she said quickly. 'I'm going to find him. He ... he wasn't feeling too good yesterday.'

Then she stopped. It was clear from Harold's face that he was worried. She could sense her cheeks flushing. 'Is there a problem?'

'Actually, yes.' He brought a large file out of the case he was carrying. 'These are the garage books. There seems to be something wrong. We're missing $15,000. Rob made these entries so I was hoping he could explain them.'

Oh no! Gail felt a cold sinking feeling in her chest. Is this why Dad was drinking? 'I'll bring him back. I'm sure there's an innocent explanation.'

Harold nodded uncertainly. 'I hope so.'

***

All the way back to Lassiters various questions kept flying through Gail's head. Did Dad really know about the missing money? But it didn't mean that he'd taken it? Did it?

The receptionist on duty – a different one from last time – gave her a knowing look as she handed her that same spare key she'd had earlier. Was the hotel aware of all the mess inside? Maybe not, as there was a Do Not Disturb sign on the door.

She knocked. No reply. Then she pushed and the door opened. It had been on the latch – that was odd. So too was the fact that all Dad's stuff was there. His clothes. The empty bottles from yesterday. But no Dad.

'No,' said the receptionist when she went back down the stairs. 'I haven't seen him.' She checked the diary. 'And he didn't come down for breakfast again.'

'Gail?' It was Paul standing beside her. 'I thought I'd come and find you.' He lowered his voice and then led her to the window for some privacy. 'Harold told me about the books. After you left, he made a few more phone calls.'

Paul was holding both her hands now. 'I'm sorry, love. But it looks as though your dad might have taken this $15,000 out of the firm.'

'Embezzlement?' she whispered.

His face was raw with sympathy. 'It's a distinct possibility.'

No. This couldn't be true.

'Where is he now?' asked Paul gently.

'That's just it,' whispered Gail. 'I don't know.'

Then she burst into tears on her husband's shoulder and felt his arms close around her comfortingly as her whole world came tumbling down.

Fifteen

PAUL

'Have a safe journey,' said Paul as he and Gail saw cousin Hilary into her car.

'Don't worry.' Their guest arranged her jacket carefully on the back seat. 'I'll be back soon. I enjoy helping people out.'

'What a cheek!' said Gail when she was out of earshot. 'Anyone would think she was doing us a favour rather than the other way round. If we hadn't put her up, she'd have had to go to the hotel, which wouldn't have been nearly as personal.'

Paul took his arm away from his wife now that Hilary's car was out of sight. 'Which was exactly why I suggested that in the first place. It was your idea to have her here.'

'I'm not going to argue.' Gail turned to go back to Number 22. 'I've got more important things on my mind. Like Dad. He must have his reasons for what he did. But I just can't think what – and he won't tell me.'

Paul sighed heavily. 'Well, we've got twenty-four hours to work it out. Otherwise Harold is going to the police.'

'No need to remind me. We've got to get it sorted by then.'

Much as he cared for Gail, there were times when he wished she'd be more realistic. 'It's not going to be enough time.'

'You don't know that! In fact ...'

But before they'd had a chance to shut the door behind them, Jim arrived. 'Has that woman gone?'

Gail gave a short laugh. 'I presume you're talking about cousin Hilary.'

'Who else? Mind if I come in for a bit?'

Not another problem?

'Why don't we have some coffee?' said Paul. 'We've got quite a few things to talk about. Gail and I are really worried about Rob.'

'Yes. We are.' Gail grabbed her bag and coat. 'In fact, I was waiting for Hilary to go before I went to look for him.'

As if on cue the doorbell rang.

'Dad!' Paul heard her scream. 'Are you all right? Paul. Come here. Quickly!'

***

For a minute, Paul had thought his new father-in-law had had a heart attack when he saw him collapsed on the ground. But as soon as he smelt Rob's breath and heard his slurred explanation, it was obvious he'd been drinking. How stupid!

Gail then told him off for being cross and said he was being 'heartless'. This led to a bit of an argument while

Rob slept it off on the sofa.

'My dad isn't a thief,' Gail had hissed.

Was she blind?

'Then sort him out,' he'd said sharply. 'I'm going into the office for some peace and quiet.'

Now, at his desk, having had time to reflect, Paul began to wonder if he'd been a bit hasty. Didn't he know from Jim that it wasn't always easy to cope with parents? Why couldn't they be the mature adults that they were meant to be?

There was a knock on the door. 'Sorry to bother you.'

Dad! Again? Of all people, his father should realise he had a business to run. 'Look, son, I've been talking to Harold. There's no getting away from it – that money is missing.'

Paul groaned. 'We already know that.'

'But I've told Harold that we don't have all the facts yet. We can't jump to conclusions. And if word of this gets out, it won't be good for business. I think Harold gets that now, so he's agreed to keep quiet about it for a bit.'

'How long is he giving us?'

'I'm not sure.'

Well at least it was something. 'Gail will be relieved.'

Jim nodded. 'You've got a great wife there.'

Right! In name only. Still, there was a lot to be said for being good friends.

***

One of the nice things about being married, Paul thought as he made his way back home after a hard day at the office, was that someone would be there waiting for him.

Okay. So he and Gail hadn't exactly seen eye to eye over Rob – he still thought there was something shifty going on there – but she was a good woman. Funny, sweet, intelligent and a great cook. Of course, their relationship was missing that essential ingredient – the bedroom – but hadn't experience shown him that wasn't everything? Even so, it would be nice to cuddle up with someone at night …

Wow. 'Something smells good,' he called out, shutting the front door behind him.

'Guess what?' Gail came running up, her cheeks flushed. 'Dad's admitted everything. You'll never believe what he did with the money.'

'So it *was* his fault?'

'Well, yes. But there's a reason. He's been gambling and now he owes $15,000.'

'How stupid is that!'

She looked awkward. 'Yes, I know. But it's all sortable, Paul. Listen! I've been to see Des.' (That was one of the advantages of having a bank manager as a neighbour.) 'And he says he'll arrange a loan for me. But he needs a guarantor. I can just about do it although my savings are pretty limited.'

Paul felt uneasy. 'I don't like the idea of you getting into debt. Let me loan it to you.'

Gail took his hands. The touch of her skin took him by surprise. They were so soft. 'That's a fantastic offer, love, but I can't take your money.'

Love? She'd never called him that before.

'You should let me help. I'm your husband, after all.'

She turned away. Instantly his hands felt empty without hers. 'Yes, but in name only.'

'Please. Even if I was just your friend, I'd offer to help.'

Gail appeared to consider this. 'Are you sure?' she asked slowly.

'Absolutely.'

Then to his relief, she nodded. 'All right. Thanks. That's really kind of you.'

For a minute he thought she was going to hug him.

'I'd better go and check on tea. Dad's coming over by the way. You don't mind, do you?'

***

The meal was not a success. Paul should have known it! Instead of being repentant, Rob spent the whole time complaining about Harold in between helping himself to more wine. He was looking dreadful. Pretty dishevelled, in fact, with red eyes. Gail had clearly noticed too and was trying to keep the bottle at their end of the table.

'At least Harold isn't going to the police yet,' Paul said.

'Course not. He's a mate, isn't he? At least I thought he was. Anyway, I thought I'd go back to work on the circuit to get some money.'

'You still haven't told us why you gambled in the first place.'

'That's right, Dad.' Gail leaned forward. She was looking particularly pretty tonight in that blue dress. 'You promised you'd put all that behind you.'

Rob shrugged. 'I don't know. Maybe it was a distraction from being lonely. Everyone else around me seems to have someone. You and Paul, you're lucky. You've got each other. Look at the two of you lovebirds!

You make a great couple. Everyone says so.'

If only he knew! Gail was going red.

'Do you want us to find somewhere bigger so you can move in with us?'

What was Gail talking about? It would be awful having Rob living with them, especially if he was going to get drunk all the time.

'No, love. I don't want to tread on your patch.'

Phew!

'Hi. Anyone in?'It was Jim, coming in through the back door from the patio. Much as Paul loved Ramsay Street, he did sometimes feel there wasn't any privacy. 'I've got some news.' He sat down at the table heavily. 'Harold's pulled out of the business.'

'Great!' Rob reached over for the bottle. 'Now we won't have that man on our backs any more.'

'Are you crazy! We'll have to pay Harold back his share now.'

'Dad's right.' Paul shot Gail a worried look.

'Well no one's going to lend me any money, are they?' said Rob, wiping his mouth. 'Not with my credit.'

'You're right.' Jim sighed. 'I'll have to see if I can come up with something instead.'

Gail leaned across and touched her father-in-law's hand. It was just a kind gesture, Paul told himself. How stupid he'd been to read anything into it when she'd done the same to him earlier. 'Thanks, Jim. That's really kind of you. Isn't it, Dad?'

Rob mumbled something and Paul felt another wave of irritation. The least the man could do was say 'thank you'.

***

Sometimes, when life all got a bit too much, the only thing to do was walk it off. Paul always loved walking round the city, especially by the river. Water was so calming. So too were bridges like this one at Lassiters. How many other people were lucky enough to have such a beautiful structure just outside their office?

Paul had often wondered about the architects and builders who had created them. Did they realise how much pleasure they were giving to future generations? Such a clever design feat too. Where did you start when you began to build a bridge? And was it any more – or less – difficult than building bridges between people?

Paul was still pondering this when he spotted the blonde woman in front of him. She looked vaguely familiar. 'Crystal?' he called out.

'Paul!'

Yes. It *was* her! And she still looked as lovely as the last time he'd seen her which was … well, ages ago. That glamorous blonde hair still curled onto her shoulders and her figure was perfect! A little over made-up perhaps but the effect was pretty stunning. Any man would be flattered to be seen with a woman like Crystal.

'How are you doing? Still modelling?'

She made a pretty little pout.

'Yeah, and I hear you're quite the big businessman these days. I reckoned that's why I hadn't heard from you for a while.'

Was she flirting with him? Paul felt an unexpected thrill go through him as they fell into step together.

'I've just been busy, that's all.' Paul was beginning to feel awkward now. Clearly she hadn't heard about his wedding or she'd have mentioned it. This was the time for him to bring up the subject but he could hardly tell her it was simply a marriage of convenience.

'Look, I've got to dash to a photographic shoot.' She was standing in front of him now. 'Why don't you give me a call sometime?'

Then, before he knew what was happening, she reached up and gave him what could only be described as a lingering kiss. Even worse, he found himself responding hungrily. It had been so long since that had happened. How much he'd missed the feel of a woman's lips!

Turning back, he watched her disappear out of sight. Should he call her? If he did, he'd have to come clean and that might be complicated ...

'Paul?'

Great! It was Gail, coming out of the office.

'Who was that blonde?' She was looking at Crystal who was still in sight, walking with that lovely stylish manner of hers as though she was on the catwalk right now.

There was no need, he told himself, to feel embarrassed, as if he'd been caught out like a cheating husband. They had an arrangement, didn't they?

'She's just someone I used to go out with.'

'I could guess that from seeing the two of you together.'

Paul shrugged. 'We're free to do what we want, aren't we?'

She nodded. 'Sure. See you back at the office. I've just nipped out to get some air.' Then she looked down at the water. 'There's something about water and bridges that's really soothing, don't you think? Oh – and don't forget the dinner party at the weekend, will you? Just in case you intend making other plans. We need to start thinking about the menu.'

***

How could he forget? The dinner was being held in honour of Mr Udagawa who was the reason that he and Gail had got married in the first place! At least it had secured the deal even if this was a mercenary way of looking at it.

'You know,' said Paul the following evening when he got back early from a meeting, 'I think we should ask all the family too. You know how much that means to our guest.'

'Sure.' Gail seemed to be avoiding his face as she spoke. 'It's good that someone appreciates traditional values, not to mention the truth.'

Was she making a dig at him about their marital arrangements? If so, that wasn't fair. She'd gone along with the wedding, hadn't she? She could have said no.

'Look.' Gail put a black box in front of him. 'I found my old flute last night while you were working late.'

She said the words 'working late' as if doubting this was what he'd actually been doing. 'Do you think Lucy would like it?'

'That's very generous of you.' Paul opened the box. The flute was in beautiful condition. 'But are you sure you really want to part with it?'

'Certain.' She snapped the box shut. 'I loved it when I was younger but I simply don't have the time now. If I had a little sister, I'd give it to her. But I don't so I'd like to give it to yours instead.'

His eyes visibly softened. 'That's really nice of you. But wouldn't you like to play it at the dinner? Mr Udagawa would love it!'

Gail turned away again. 'Don't overdo it with this "hostess" thing!'

'There's no need to be so sharp.'

'I'm not.' Despite her words, she turned back again as if she was sorry. 'Got any plans for tonight?'

He glanced at his watch. 'Actually, yes. That's one reason why I'm back early.'

'I see. Want to eat something first?'

'No thanks.'

'Fine.'

Oh dear. 'Have you cooked something special?'

'Nothing that can't keep.' She began tidying up some magazines on the table although they seemed quite neat as they were.

'I can cancel my arrangements,' he said quickly.

'There's no need to do that.'

She was standing up now, with a smile on her face. Just like the kind of smile they had both learned to use at the airline when there was a difficult passenger who had to be controlled but still treated in a civil fashion. 'We both said we were free to lead our own lives when we got married, didn't we? In fact, I've got plans too.'

'Really?'

'Yes, Paul. You don't think you're the only one to have a social life, do you?'

'No. But …'

'Great. Then I'll see you later tonight – or maybe tomorrow morning.'

Paul felt an uneasy flutter in his chest. For a moment,

he really wished he was having dinner with Gail and not with Crystal. Besides, if he wasn't mistaken, that had been quite a sad look on his wife's face when she'd turned away just then. Was it possible that she felt the same?

No. Don't be so silly. If Gail really felt something for him, she'd have told him. Besides, a man couldn't live like a hermit for the rest of his life, could he? And Crystal had made it very clear that she found him very attractive. In fact, her attention was pretty flattering!

Sixteen

GAIL

Gail spotted Lucy walking past the house just as she was about to leave for work.

'Hi,' she called out. 'Can you hang on for a second? I want to give you something!'

Lucy turned back with that sunny smile on her face. She might be a handful sometimes, according to the Robinsons, but she looked so sweet in her school uniform. In some ways she reminded Gail of herself at that age. So young and innocent. Maybe it was just as well she hadn't known then what life had in store for her. Hopefully Lucy would never have to go through the same pain.

'We thought you might like my old flute. Look!' Gail dashed back inside for a second. 'I was going to bring it round later but why don't you have it now?'

'Wow!' Lucy opened the box right there on the doorstep. 'It's amazing. Thank you so much.'

Gail felt a lovely warm feeling surging through her

heart. 'Just make sure you keep up with your lessons – not like me. I'm afraid I wasn't as conscientious as I should have been.'

'I will! Honestly!' Lucy gave Gail a big hug. 'Especially now I've got this. It's so much nicer than my old one.'

'I'm glad it's found a new home. Much better than sitting at the back of my wardrobe. Listen, why don't you come over tonight? Then you can play it for us.'

'I'd love to. I could come after my music lesson.'

'That's fine.'

'Gail!' It was Paul standing by their car in the street. 'Hurry up or I'll be late for my meeting.'

She raised her eyebrows. 'Better do what the boss says.'

Lucy giggled. Then she gave her another hug round her waist. 'I love having you in our family, Gail.'

What a lovely thing to say. Gail's heart gave another little flip as she watched Lucy run off to school with her old flute tucked under her arm. How wonderful it would be to have a daughter like that one day …

'I can see someone's a fan,' said Paul as she finally got into the car.

Gail nodded happily as she put her seat belt on. 'I really like being part of your family.'

Paul gently touched her cheek. For a moment, Gail couldn't help feeling a little tremor. There were times when she forgot that their marriage was a sham. What would it be like, she wondered, if Paul showed a bit more affection?

Then she shook herself. Don't be silly. That wasn't the arrangement. Besides, this way, they knew exactly where they stood. And no one could get hurt.

Work was full on that day. So many meetings to organise and decisions to be made. Gail still hadn't finished when Paul put his head round the door. 'I'm just going to shower at Lassiters.'

Of course. His date with Crystal! Gail felt that strange tremble in her chest again.

'It's not too late for me to cancel, if you like.'

Instantly Gail put a smile on her face. 'Don't do it for my sake. In fact, I've got dinner plans too. You go ahead and have a good time.'

'You too.'

For a minute, he looked as though he was going to come a bit nearer to her. But no. 'See you later.'

What else did you expect, Gail asked herself. Wasn't this what they had decided before tying the knot? Separate lives. Anyway, she'd better get moving herself or she wouldn't be ready for Lucy.

***

It was just before 6 p.m. when the phone rang.

'Gail, love?' It was Jim. 'Look, I'm really sorry but Lucy can't come to you after all. Says she's feeling sick. Must have eaten something off, I think, although she hasn't been vomiting or anything like that.' His voice sounded worried. 'Poor kid. She was so excited about coming to you. Maybe you'd like to come over here instead.'

'Sure.'

It didn't take Gail long to run a brush through her hair. 'How's Lucy feeling?' she asked as soon as she got to Number 26.

Jim put a finger to his lips. 'She's on the sofa. Says she doesn't want to talk. In fact, I'm wondering if she's actually upset about something rather than being sick.'

That didn't sound good. Maybe someone had been bullying her at school. Gail could remember pretending to be ill when one of the girls in class had been really nasty because Gail had been chosen for the running team and her rival hadn't.

'Hi. How did your flute lesson go?'

'I had to miss it.' Lucy turned away. 'Didn't feel well.'

She looked all right. In fact, her face was quite pink. Gail opened her bag. 'Look. I've brought over our wedding pictures. Thought you might like to look at them with me.'

But to her surprise, Lucy jumped up. 'I'm going to my room.'

Had she just done something to upset her?

'Don't worry,' said Helen, who had come into the room just in time to witness Lucy running off. 'She's probably had another quarrel with Emma or one of her other friends. You know what girls can be like.'

But Gail wasn't so sure. That look on Lucy's face just now had been directed at her. Was it possible that she knew something that she shouldn't ...?

'Are you sure I haven't upset her?' Gail asked.

'What on earth could you have done?' said Helen. 'Lucy adores you. Keeps saying how "great" you are.' She held out her hand. 'In fact, we all think the same.'

Gail flushed. If only they knew! 'Hopefully Lucy will feel better by tomorrow night. For the dinner with the Udagawas.'

'Ah.' Helen looked awkward. 'I'm afraid I can't make that after all. So sorry but something has come up which I can't get out of.'

That wasn't good news. 'I just hope the dinner goes well,' said Gail nervously. 'This deal is so important.'

'You and Paul have been so worried about this man! I know it means a lot to the business, but I don't think you have anything to worry you. Your client is thrilled that the two of you have got married. In fact, you couldn't have done anything better if you'd tried.'

But that's just the trouble, Gail thought as she went back to her place. They *had* tried. More than anyone else realised.

'Paul?' she called out when she got home. 'Are you back?'

But the lights weren't on even though the radio was still playing merrily in the kitchen: just as she had left it.

In all likelihood, Paul and Crystal would still be having dinner. Or maybe another drink in the bar. Or perhaps they were …

No. Don't think about that, Gail told herself sharply. And anyway, even if they were doing *that*, it was Paul's business. After all, he was only her husband in name. Just as they'd agreed.

***

'Morning!' said Gail, looking up from the kitchen counter where she was whipping up a couple of eggs. 'Did you have a good evening?'

She was still in her nightie even though she'd woken really early that morning, wondering if Paul had actually come home. From the look of him, tousled hair and dressing gown, he had. An unexpected flash of relief went through her.

'Very nice thanks.'

Nice? That didn't sound very passionate! Maybe he was downplaying it for her feelings.

'Fancy an omelette?'

'No thanks.' He rubbed his eyes. 'I had a bit too much to drink last night. I couldn't eat anything at the moment.'

Gail turned back to the oven to hide her face.

'How was your evening?' he asked behind her.

'Actually,' she said, flipping the omelette over even though she'd already done that twice, 'I think something's up with Lucy. I'm pretty certain I've upset her.'

'That can't be right. She thinks the world of you.'

'I'm not so sure.' Gail felt composed enough now to take her omelette to the breakfast bar and join Paul who had made himself a mug of black coffee. 'Something's going on but I don't know what. Also, your gran can't make the dinner with Mr Udagawa.'

'No!'

'Not great, is it. I was wondering if we should ask Dad instead to make up numbers.'

Paul was shaking his head. 'I don't think it's a good idea. You've got to admit it, love. He's not in a good place at the moment.'

Love? Was that what he had called Crystal too? Or maybe it was something more passionate …

'We can't afford any mistakes tonight,' continued Paul.

Gail got up, her breakfast still half-finished. 'You

make it all sound so clinical.'

Paul shrugged. 'That's business, isn't it?'

'Yes.' Her voice was cool. 'You're right. See you later.'

'Where are you going?'

She shrugged. 'Just out.'

If he could play at that game, so could she.

***

'Hi love,' said Rob when she got to the garage.

He didn't look very pleased to see her. First Lucy and now her father! He looked up from the workbench where he and Jim were huddled together. Looked as though they'd been talking about something pretty important. Probably the missing money. Another thing to worry about.

'Come to talk about anything in particular, have you?'

This wasn't like Dad. Mind you, he hadn't been himself since she'd found out about the gambling. No doubt he was ashamed of himself – as well he might be.

'Just came round to say hello actually, but I can see you're busy.'

'We're talking work, I'm afraid,' said Jim.

Clearly they didn't want her around.

'I'll see you tonight, shall I?' he added.

Gail had been hoping he wouldn't mention that in front of Dad.

Rob's face sharpened. 'What's happening tonight?'

Oh oh.

'Just a dinner for Mr Udagawa and his wife. She's just flown in to join him.'

'And you didn't think to ask your old dad?'

'It's business. But you're welcome to come if you want.'

'No thanks.'

This was awful! It was clear that he felt left out.

'Please.' She went up to give him a hug. 'I want you to.'

He moved away. 'Then you should have given me more notice. Anyway, you probably don't want a drunken gambler like me around to mess things up.'

'That's not why …'

'Forget it. You go off and start cooking. Jim and I have got things to talk about.'

This was all Paul's fault, Gail thought angrily as she left. He should have agreed to ask Dad. Hadn't they always said that family was more important than anything? But maybe Crystal had made him change his mind.

***

'Smells delicious,' said Paul.

'I hope it tastes as good.'

Gail put the final touches to the starter and then checked the table to make sure she hadn't left anything out. She had a feeling that Mrs Udagawa might be a bit of a perfectionist on the home front, just like her husband was at work.

'It looks beautiful,' said Paul. 'I like the way you've folded the napkins. And the candles are a nice touch.'

Gail couldn't help feeling nervous. So much depended on this!

'It will be all right.' Paul touched her arm lightly. 'You look lovely by the way. Those trousers suit you.

Are they new?'

'Actually they were a present.'

'Really?'

She could tell that he wanted to ask who gave them to her. No need to mention that she'd actually used a voucher which an aunt had sent for her last birthday.

'There's the door!' Gail said quickly. 'He's here. You go!'

'We must both go.' Paul took her arm properly this time. 'Or he'll think it's odd.'

The Udagawas had clearly dressed for a more formal occasion. Maybe Paul should have worn a suit too! Mrs Udagawa looked extremely neat and chic in her suit. Perhaps a dress might have been more appropriate than these trousers! Still, it was too late to change.

'Welcome to our home,' said Gail quickly as Paul ushered in their guests.

Mr Udagawa bowed. 'We are very honoured.' Then he held out a package. 'Please accept this as a token of our esteem. It is a Japanese wedding blessing scroll.'

Gail could hardly look at her husband as she unrolled it.

'How very beautiful! Thank you. What does the writing say?'

'It is to bring you luck.' Mrs Udagawa looked first at her and then at Paul and then back at her. It was almost as if she was checking they were really a couple. 'With all the best wishes for the future.'

'Thank you.' Paul was already taking down a picture in the hall and hanging the blessing on it instead. 'We are very grateful.'

'Hello!' They must have left the door ajar – it was Jim

and Lucy. 'I'm so sorry that Helen couldn't come but …'

'What's that?' asked Lucy, looking at the scroll on the wall.

'It's a wedding blessing,' said Paul. 'Mr and Mrs Udagawa have just given it to us. Isn't it lovely?'

Lucy said nothing.

I'm right, thought Gail. There really is something wrong.

'Please,' she said quickly, to avoid the awkwardness which was hanging in the air. 'Do come and sit down. I thought you might like to look at our wedding photographs over drinks before we eat.'

'That would be very nice.' Mrs Udagawa sat very precisely on the edge of the sofa. 'What a lovely home you have.'

'Thank you. I lived here with my father until Paul and I got married. Then he moved to the hotel.'

'Really?' There was a distinct note of disapproval there from Mrs Udagawa. 'In our country, elderly relatives often continue to live with us.'

Oh dear. Swiftly, Gail opened the wedding album as a distraction.

Then Mrs Udagawa turned to Lucy. 'You are very quiet. Do you not like looking at photographs?'

'Not these.'

How rude!

'I'm afraid Lucy hasn't been feeling very well recently.'

'I'm fine now.'

What was going on?

'Would you excuse us? Lucy is just going to help me

put the meal out.'

'I didn't say that ...'

'Hello, everyone! I'm here. Even though you didn't invite me.'

Oh no! It was Dad. And he was clearly drunk, judging from the way he was ranting and swaying. The Udagawas were looking at him with undisguised horror.

Paul was trying to steady his new father-in-law. 'Nice to see you, Rob. And you're wrong. We did want to invite you but ...'

'No you didn't.' He grabbed Mrs Udagawa's hand and she let out a little grimace. Then he put his face really close to hers. 'My daughter thought I might embarrass you. Well, you know what? I don't care if I do. You'll still give them your business won't you?'

'Please, Dad,' blustered Gail.

'Let's get you settled in the guest room,' said Paul.

'I'm not going to any guest room.' Rob pushed him away. 'I want to be here with everyone else.'

'QUIET, EVERYONE!'

Lucy! Everyone was staring at her now.

'What's wrong, love,' said Gail trying to cuddle her.

'Go away. And you too, Paul. I don't trust either of you. Or anyone else in the room. Not after ...'

Then she burst into tears.

'I think it would be best if we left,' said Mr Udagawa, taking his wife's arm.

Their dinner party was ruined. So too – in all likelihood – was their business deal.

'Maybe we can speak tomorrow?' asked Paul in a quiet voice.

Mr Udagawa merely stared at him. Then he made his

own way to the front door with Paul hotly in pursuit, trying to make him change his mind.

'Have I messed up again?' slurred Rob.

Yes. He had. But it was Lucy – who had run back home – who Gail was really worried about. Blow the business deal and the Udagawas! It was her new family that really mattered.

Seventeen

PAUL

How could the dinner party have gone so wrong, Paul asked himself as he sat in the kitchen, nursing a cup of coffee. First, Lucy had been so rude and offhand to him. And then his father-in-law bursting in when he was so drunk.

It couldn't have been worse if they'd tried. No wonder Mr Udagawa had called off the deal. He'd made it plain from the start that family was very important to him. 'You must understand that I cannot do business with you now,' he'd said coolly before leaving last night.

Paul's thoughts were suddenly interrupted by a soft padding down the stairs. 'I'm so sorry about Dad,' said Gail. How embarrassing! He was still in his pyjamas. Then again, it was only 6.30 a.m. Even so, Gail was neatly dressed in a crisp white shirt with cropped trousers. How lovely and fresh she smelt. As if she had just stepped out of the shower.

'I couldn't sleep all night,' she continued, helping

herself to a mug. 'I can't believe my father's behaviour. And what do you think is going on with Lucy?'

Paul shrugged. Frankly, his little sister was the least of their problems in the scale of things. 'No idea. All I do know is that I've just lost what might have been the biggest deal of my life.'

Gail laid a hand on his arm. 'Is it definitely over?'

He nodded, not trusting himself to say any more in case he said something terrible about Rob. Gail might be cross with him too but he was still her dad.

'Did you know your father told my dad that they'll have to sell the garage?' asked Gail. 'He's pretty cut up about it.'

'Well I'm pretty cut up about losing the deal,' retorted Paul.

'How do you think I feel?' Gail rounded on him. 'It's not my fault.'

'I didn't say it was …'

'Children can't take the blame for their parents' behaviour any more than parents can take the blame for the way their kids turn out.'

'I'm not sure about that.' Paul suddenly felt the need for some space. 'Look, I'm going round to see Gran. See you later. Okay?'

***

'I tell you, Dad. It's true.'

Paul heard Lucy's angry voice as soon as he arrived.

'What's true?'

His father looked awkward. 'It's nothing.'

'Yes it is.' Lucy's face had two pink spots on each cheek, the way it always did when she was upset.

'Emma and I saw you kissing another woman the other night.' Her eyes were glistening with fury. 'How could you cheat on Gail? You've only just got married and she's so nice.'

Paul felt his heart sink. 'It's not quite what you think …'

His voice faltered as he tried desperately to come up with some plausible excuse. 'Crystal – the woman you saw – is an old friend. A sort of business contact.'

'Sort of?' repeated Jim, his eyebrows raised.

'Yes.' Paul made himself sound firm. 'She's the kind of woman who likes to show affection.'

'Hah!' snorted Lucy. 'That was clear. I suppose you're going to say there's nothing in it.'

'There isn't.' Paul felt as though he was trying to convince himself as well as his dad and Lucy. 'If you don't believe me, ask Gail. I told her all about it.'

Lucy frowned. 'Really? Even the kiss?'

'Absolutely. We tell each other everything.'

Well, that was almost true.

'Tell you what,' he continued. 'Why don't you come over to our place and ask her yourself?'

'Right now?' Lucy had her hands on both hips as though she was a teacher and he was a kid again.

'Sure.'

'Okay.' Lucy glanced down at her pyjamas. 'I'll just go and get ready.'

Jim waited until she'd left the room. 'Right. Are you going to tell me the truth?'

Paul forced himself to look him straight in the eyes, hating himself as he did so. 'It is the truth. Gail does know about Crystal. I wouldn't cheat on her. Honestly. I

… I love her.'

'I hope so.' Jim shook his head. 'Because if you ask me, Gail is the best thing that has happened to this family for a long time. And I wouldn't want to see her hurt again after everything she's been through.'

A twinge went through Paul. 'Nor would I. Believe me. Look, I'll see you later. I need to get back to my place.'

'But you've only just come over.'

'Yes … well … I've just thought of something I need to tell Gail.'

Jim gave him a sceptical glance. 'Does it concern this Crystal by any chance?'

'No. It's business. She's pretty cut up about you selling the garage, you know. It's going to put Rob in a tricky position.'

'Then he should have thought about that before he started stealing money and messing up business deals. Just as you need to think carefully about kissing women in public when you've only just got married, son.'

***

What a mess! If Dad and Lucy knew the truth, what would they think? Paul didn't even want to consider that. Right now, he needed to rush back and warn Gail about Lucy coming over. She was cleaning out kitchen cupboards when he rushed in.

Briefly, he outlined the situation. 'I see.' Gail was looking at him quizzically. 'So what exactly do you want me to say?'

Paul had one eye on the door as he spoke. Lucy might be coming in any minute! 'That there's nothing between me and Crystal.'

'And is that what you told *her*? Your girlfriend, that is.'

Paul was beginning to feel a bit fed up now. They'd written the rules together, hadn't they? 'That's my business. Remember what we said? We'd each live independent lives without asking questions.'

Gail got back down on the floor again and began scrubbing away at a bottom cupboard. He couldn't see her face but he could guess what she was feeling from the tone. 'I'm not going to lie to Lucy.'

'I'm not asking you to but …'

'Gail!' Lucy flew in without knocking. Running up to Gail, she wrapped her arms round her waist. 'Paul says there's nothing between him and this woman I saw. He says you knew about her and that she's just one of these people who … who likes to show affection. Is that right?'

She was looking up at Gail now beseechingly. His wife – it still felt so strange to use that word – stared unflinchingly at him above Lucy's little head. 'Actually …'

Paul held his breath.

'Actually, it *is* true. Your brother was very honest with me.'

'Really?' Lucy clearly wasn't giving up so easily.

'Really. We're very happy, aren't we, Paul?'

He tried to speak but his throat was dry. 'Very,' he managed to croak.

'But you never show each other much affection. You don't keep kissing and that kind of stuff like you see on television.'

'That's because we're not young kids any more.'

Lucy's laugh appeared to have a touch of sarcasm to it.

'And just because we don't kiss all the time doesn't mean we don't love each other,' added Paul. Then on impulse, he went up to Gail and dropped a kiss on top of her head.

That was better. Lucy looked more convinced even though Gail seemed a bit taken aback by his action.

'Ugh! If you're going to start kissing, I'm leaving!'

Paul tried to make a joke out of it. 'There's no pleasing you. First I don't kiss my wife enough and then I do it too much.'

Lucy ran back to Gail for another cuddle. 'Sorry I got it wrong but I really love you. And I don't want to see you upset.'

Gail bent down to cuddle the child. 'I really love you too. Why don't you come back later and bring your flute?'

'Great!' Those pink spots were shining. 'Thanks so much.' Then she skipped happily out of the house, singing as she went.

'So,' said Gail sharply when the door had shut. 'Did I play my part all right?'

He nodded. 'Yes. Thanks.'

But inside, he felt that old twinge of doubt running through him. This was awful! He felt like a total imposter and he could see that Gail felt like one too.

***

They spent the rest of the day pottering round the house and doing the kind of jobs – like vacuuming and hosing down the patio – that married couples do. Except that they weren't married, were they? Not really. Only on paper. Still, that's what they'd agreed.

But how long could they keep this up in front of other people? Speaking of whom, he was due to speak to Mr Udagawa just before he left for Japan. Better get the call over and done with.

It didn't take long.

'Who were you talking to on the phone just then?' asked Gail when he came back into the kitchen.

'It wasn't Crystal, if that's what you were thinking.'

'I wasn't. And even if I was, it would be none of my business.'

That was true.

'Actually, I was talking to Mr Udagawa to see if there was any chance he might change his mind.'

'And is there?'

'I'm afraid not. He's adamant. In fact, he kept repeating that a good business could only be run by a united family and that we clearly weren't what he thought we were.' He bit his lip. 'The thing is that Rosemary is going to be furious when she finds out about it. She's bound to think badly of me. She might even decide to fly over and give me a hard time.'

'But it wasn't your fault.' Gail reached for his hand and gave it a quick squeeze. 'In fact, I feel responsible because it was my dad. And to think we only got married to secure the deal.'

Paul's heart began to beat heavily. 'Do you want to get divorced then?'

Her eyes looked up at him. 'Do you?'

'No.' He said the word with more force than he meant

to. 'We didn't just get married because of the deal, if you remember. We did it for convenience.'

'Ah, yes. Convenience.'

Paul began to fluster. 'You know. So we wouldn't be pestered by other people ...'

'Like Crystal.'

'Yes ... and because it would make us financially secure.'

'Very practical.' Her voice was clipped and tight.

'It's what we both agreed.'

'I know. But if the Japanese deal had gone ahead ...'

'I'm really sorry about messing it up,' cut in a familiar voice.

He and Gail both whipped round as Rob appeared through the back door. What else had he overheard?

Rob just walked in and sat down on a chair as if the place was still his. 'Is there anything I can do to put things right?'

'No,' said Paul tightly. 'There isn't. The deal is off.'

'Thanks, Dad.' Gail waved her hand as if she was batting him away. 'You've no right to come barging into our home. You did enough damage when you did that the other night.'

Rob rubbed his chin ruefully. 'That's why I'm here. To say sorry again.'

With any luck, Paul told himself, his father-in-law hadn't overheard anything else. Or else, with a mouth like his, he'd surely say something.

'Nothing you can do will make any difference, Dad.'

'But you didn't mean it, love, did you, when you said after the party that you never wanted to see me again?'

Paul almost felt sorry for his father-in-law. He sounded

like a child.

Gail hesitated. 'No, but I do need a bit of a break. I want you gone. Get it?'

Both men stared at her as she swept off. 'That's not like my Gail,' said Rob quietly.

Honestly. Paul had really had enough now. 'You've got to see her point. You didn't just mess up my deal, you embarrassed your daughter. If you really want to say sorry, you'll show it by sorting out your life. And not upsetting Gail. Now, if you don't mind, please leave. We need some time to ourselves.'

It was true. There was nothing Paul wanted more than to sit down with Gail or maybe go for a walk in the park with her after their conversation just now. But here was Lucy! 'Is Gail ready?' she demanded.

'For what?'

'Our flute practice, of course.'

He'd forgotten. And so, he wouldn't mind betting, had Gail.

'We're ready!' Gail came flying down the stairs. Her face was smiley and she looked nothing like the woman who had just told her own father to leave. 'Aren't we, darling?'

Darling? Was she really speaking to him? Of course, she was. They needed to put on a show for Lucy, didn't they?

***

'Thanks for a great time.' Lucy looked at both of them as she put away her flute. Her eyes narrowed. 'You're sure you two are okay?'

Paul put an arm around Gail. 'Of course we are.'

'Well just be careful.' Lucy was wagging a finger bossily. 'Or else Gail might decide to go and kiss someone else if you're not nice to her.'

Paul laughed. 'I don't think that will happen, will it, darling?'

'I don't know!' Gail's eyes were sparkling. 'I might think about it if you don't behave. Don't worry, Lucy, I'm only joking.'

'I know you are.' Lucy gave Gail another hug. 'See you tomorrow. Bye!'

Paul stood at the window watching his little sister run down the street back to her place. 'Phew. I think we sorted that one out. Thanks, Gail. You're one in a million.' Then he turned. 'Sorry. I didn't realise you were behind me.'

She was so close that he could smell her scent. Instinctively, he reached down to give her a kiss on her cheek. But instead, his mouth found hers. Wow! She was kissing him back. Paul found his hands cupping the back of her head as the kiss grew more and more passionate. This was amazing. In fact, he'd never known anything like this before …

'What are we doing?' gasped Gail, breaking away.

'I don't know.' Paul felt a crashing disappointment at her words. For a minute then, he had thought … What exactly, *had* he thought?

'We can't let this happen again,' she continued.

'No. Of course not.' Taking her lead, he rushed on. 'Strictly business – just like we agreed.'

'Exactly.'

'Still, at least Lucy's happy.'

'True.'

'Hello!' called out a voice. 'Anyone in?'

Wasn't anyone going to give them some peace and quiet?

'Hi, Helen.' Gail sounded pleased to hear her. Maybe she was glad of the interruption. 'Come on in.'

Gran – elegant as ever – gave them both a warm hug. 'Don't want to interrupt you two lovebirds but I wondered if you could do us a favour. Paul – your dad needs some help cutting down a tree in the backyard.'

'Sure.' He gave Gail a pointed look. 'We weren't doing anything, were we?'

'No. Not at all.'

'I also wanted to apologise for not being at the dinner for the Udagawas.' Helen gave a sigh. 'I heard all about Rob ...'

Gail gave a little noise.

'I'm sorry, dear. I believe Mr Udagawa is flying back to Japan later today.'

'You didn't tell me that,' said Gail quickly.

Paul shrugged. 'Doesn't make any difference now when he goes back, does it?'

Helen nodded. 'Only way to look at it. I only hope that Rosemary sees it that way.'

'Just what I'm worried about.' There was an awkward silence. Come on, Paul told himself. Pull yourself together. 'Let's get on with that tree, shall we?'

'Good idea.' Helen gave him a pat on the back. 'It will take your mind off things.'

***

By the time Paul came back, he was hungry. Thirsty too. That tree hadn't been easy! Still, it was all done now.

Maybe Gail and he could have a nice quiet dinner together at home. Yet the thought of that kiss was still playing on his mind ...

'Hi.' Gail looked up from the kitchen table where she was painting her nails. 'Tea's in the fridge.'

'Great. Thanks. What are we having?'

'What are *you* having, you mean! I'm going out.'

Paul felt a tremor of unease. 'Really? Where?'

He only just stopped himself from adding the words, 'and with who?'

Gail held up her right hand for inspection, blowing on her nails. 'I think that's my business, don't you?'

'Sure. Of course.'

Gail was examining her left hand now. She didn't normally go for dark red.

'See you later then.' Briefly she brushed his cheek and he caught a whiff of perfume: the one she only wore for best.

Then she stood at the door, looking for all the world like a model on a magazine front cover. Gorgeous Gail. That's what they used to call her at the airline. But in those days, he had felt differently about her. Now he'd learned to get to know the real Gail. At least, he thought he had.

'Bye!' She waved her hand. 'Oh and don't bother to wait up. Not sure when I'll be back.'

Where was she going? And, more importantly, who was she meeting? Paul stared through the window as he watched Gail get into her car. Suddenly he didn't feel hungry any more ...

Eighteen

GAIL

'Mr Udagawa!' exclaimed Gail as her office door opened. 'Thank you for coming.'

Her visitor bowed his head without saying anything.

'I'm so sorry.' Nerves made Gail speak much faster than usual. 'If I could just explain about last night …'

Still silence.

Oh dear. This was going to be harder than she'd thought. 'I'm afraid my father was drunk because he's about to lose his business. Both Paul and I are mortified by his terrible behaviour. Please reconsider your decision. This deal means so much to us both.'

At last! He was looking up at her – but with a surprised expression. 'I think you have misunderstood me. I was not upset by your father's "terrible" behaviour but I *was* shocked that you and your husband did not show him respect. Loyalty is very important in my country. Parents should be revered at all cost. How can I trust the pair of you if you cannot even be loyal to your own family?'

Gail sank down on a chair, almost too upset to talk. 'You're right,' she said eventually. 'But, to be honest, I have been through so much with Dad. He has embarrassed us on many occasions but now I can see we've been wrong. We should have been more understanding. I'm so sorry but I'm also grateful to you. Sometimes it takes an outsider to point out home truths like this.' She raised her head. 'I love my father. I really do.'

Mr Udagawa's face softened. 'I can see that. I also see that you want to please both your father and your husband. It is not an easy road to follow. Perhaps I have been too harsh myself. I will sign the contract after all.'

***

'Thank goodness for that!' whooped Paul when Gail told him.

'I know. I'm relieved too. But you know what? I also feel ashamed about not making more allowances for Dad. It's a big blow losing the business.'

'Maybe we could try and help him find another job. Let's discuss it tonight at home.'

When he said it like that, it felt so cosy – as if they were a normal married couple looking forward to some time together after work.

But her relief was short-lived. When she got back home there was a letter from Dad. This didn't feel good. Dad hardly ever wrote to her. There was no need when they lived so close. They either called each other or popped round instead.

'What does he say?' asked Paul.

Gail's voice was choked. 'Dad thinks he's let us down. He thinks it's best if he leaves Erinsborough and has signed his share of the garage over to Jim.'

'What?'

Just then the phone went.

'Maybe it's him!'

Paul grabbed the receiver. 'Hello? Right. I see. That's marvellous. Thank you very much.'

'Was that Dad?' burst out Gail as he put the receiver down. 'I wanted to talk to him.'

Paul's eyes were shining. 'Actually, it was Mr Udagawa. He wants me to come over to his hotel room now and sign on the dotted line.'

Gail turned away. 'I don't care about the stupid deal now. I just want to get my dad back. What if he's sitting in some seedy motel room, drinking himself to death over his sorrows?'

'I know it's a worry.' Paul put an arm around her shoulders but Gail found herself shrugging him off.

'It's not my fault, love.'

'I didn't say it was,' she snapped. 'And don't call me "love".'

'Fine.' Paul put on his jacket. 'I'll be back as soon as I can although I might be taking Mr Udagawa out to dinner to celebrate. Do you want to join us?'

'Celebrate? After Dad's taken himself off goodness knows where? Are you joking?'

While he was out, Gail spent most of the evening ringing round to try and get hold of her dad. But no one knew where he was.

Finally there was the click of the key in the lock. But it was Paul. 'Back so soon?'

'I told him I wanted to return to my wife. He seemed to approve. Listen.' Paul took both her hands. This time she didn't push him away. 'I can see you're clearly unhappy. I don't want that so I'm willing to let you go. Now that the deal is in the bag with Udagawa, we can see a solicitor and end the marriage. I'll give you a settlement and we can live our own lives honestly in the open.'

Why did her heart fall even though this made perfect sense? 'I'm not sure,' she said slowly. 'If we get a divorce now it would really hurt your family. And I've really grown to love them.'

'And they love you.' Paul was still holding her hands. 'Look, I won't pressurise you into making a decision. Just think about it. That's all.'

***

The following evening, Scott and Charlene came round. To be honest, thought Gail, she'd rather cancel it after everything that had been going on but it would only be awkward.

'We've got this great board game,' giggled Charlene. 'It's to see how much couples know about each other.'

What? Gail and Paul both looked at each other in horror.

'Okay. So who was Gail's best friend at school, Paul?'

'Er …'

'Actually, I didn't have one,' butted in Gail quickly. 'I was part of a big group.'

'That's right.' Paul was floundering around desperately. 'Susie and Katy, wasn't it? And Emily, I believe?'

'Got it in one!'

'Well done, Paul! What about you, Gail. What big event happened to Paul when he was six?'

This was impossible! Suddenly, a memory came back to her of something which *she* had done at that age.

'He, er, he broke his arm?'

'Almost! He broke a leg falling out of a tree. You'll have to listen to your new husband's childhood stories more carefully, Gail! Here, let me help you take those glasses into the kitchen.'

He was such a nice young man!

'You know,' Scott said, as they loaded up the dishwasher, 'I'm so glad that my big brother has found love at last. He hasn't had an easy ride.'

'No,' said Gail slowly. 'He hasn't.'

'You're the perfect woman for him. You're softening that tough part of him, you know.'

'Really?'

'Yes. We can all see it.'

Well she couldn't!

'And I really appreciate the support you've given us. Charlene and I know that everyone thinks we're too young. But I overheard Paul saying that you thought we were good together and that there was no reason why a teenage marriage shouldn't work.'

'That's true.' Gail could hardly speak, thanks to the big lump which had come up in her throat.

'Charlene and I were talking the other night about how you define love. What do you think?''

This was awful!

'I'm not sure really.' She hesitated. 'I suppose it's when two people really care for each other and are prepared to battle through the difficult times as well as the good. They've also got to be totally honest with each other.'

Scott's eyes were shining! 'That's exactly what Charlene and I said! I just know we're all going to get on really well.'

How could she go on with this charade, Gail asked herself as they went back to join the others. Scott and his family were so lovely. She hated deceiving them in this way.

***

'Phew,' breathed Paul after they'd left. 'That was tough going, wasn't it?'

'Quite funny too.' Despite the worry about her father, Gail couldn't help feeling rather wistful. 'They are so in love, aren't they? I remember feeling that way about Jeremy.'

'Me too, with Terry.'

Paul went quiet for a minute. Gail shivered. The trauma at the end of his marriage was as horrendous as her own. Never did she want to go through the same pain and grief and loss again. Nor would she wish it on her worst enemy, let alone Paul, who was fast becoming a good friend.

'Aren't we lucky then,' she said quickly,' that we're both in a partnership where we can't be hurt.'

'Exactly.' He patted her shoulder. 'Maybe you were right earlier about staying put. There's something quite comforting about having all the advantages of marriage and none of the disadvantages. Don't you think?'

***

The postcard was in the mail box when Gail got up after over-sleeping. Thank goodness!

'I just need time to sort myself out, love. Please don't worry about me. I'll be back.'

That was something. At least he was safe and also in touch with her. Yet Mr Udagawa's words about respect kept haunting her mind. How she wished that she and Dad could have parted on better terms.

'Look,' she said waving the card in front of Paul who was just coming in with a bag of groceries and some delicious-smelling bread and a bag of fruit.

'Great news!' Paul handed her a fresh peach. 'I've got something to tell you too. I went into the estate agents on the way back and told them I was looking for a new place.'

Gail's heart thumped. 'Why? I thought we'd agreed to stay together for the time being.'

'As a couple, yes. But this house … well, look at it.' Paul waved his hand around. 'It's too small for entertaining.'

Gail's relief about staying together was now replaced by apprehension. It was like a familiar rug being pulled from under her feet. 'But I love Ramsay Street. And I like having your family so nearby.'

Her mind flashed back to all those lonely evenings after the divorce and the uncertainty of life ahead. At least now she had a solid base again. How could Paul take that away from her?

'Don't you see?' She tugged at his arm. 'After everything that's happened to me, I need some stability.' A big lump came into her throat. 'This house gives me roots.'

'And you'll put them down somewhere new – somewhere better!' For a minute, she almost thought he was going to give her a hug but then he stepped back. 'The estate agent is going to look out some places for us. We can start viewing tomorrow!'

'I don't know,' she murmured.

'Honestly, Gail. I think a change of scene is just what we need. That game of Scott and Charlene's really brought it home to me. We hardly know anything about each other's old lives apart from a few basic facts. But a new house will help us build a fresh future together without any strings attached.'

Nineteen

PAUL

Nearly a week had passed, during which Paul purposely hadn't mentioned moving house again. Gail's speech the other day had really moved him. Until then, he hadn't fully understood how much stability meant to her. Or how much it meant to him too …

'I thought we'd go for a little drive after work today,' he said, coming into the office.

'Really?' She looked up from her pile of papers. 'I've got a lot to get through here. To be honest, I was thinking of working late.'

'Come on. You deserve a rest after everything you've been through.'

Her face fell as if he'd reminded her of something which she'd been trying to put to the back of her mind. 'I haven't heard any more from Dad. Suppose something's happened to him?'

Paul shook his head. There were times when he really wanted to shake some sense into his father-in-law.

Didn't he realise how much he'd upset his daughter? 'He'll be fine. Remember what his postcard said. He just needs some space. Now how about that drive? It will give you a break.'

Gail nodded. 'Maybe you're right.'

'Great. The truth is, Gail, that I've found the perfect house for us and I just know you're going to agree.'

She looked worried. 'What if I don't?'

'Then I won't push you. Promise. The decision has to be yours.'

'Okay. Thanks.'

He could almost hear his heart beating as they got into the car. If he hadn't bumped into a certain person soon after their last conversation, he might never have thought of the idea. But supposing Gail didn't like it? Sometimes it was so hard to know how women's minds worked! After all, he hadn't got it right with Terry and look what had happened then … No. He wouldn't allow himself to think about it. This was Gail's moment.

'But we're outside our own house,' exclaimed Gail. 'Have you left something behind?'

'No.' Paul reached into the glove compartment for the black box which he'd been keeping secret. 'Go on. Open it!'

'A key!'

'That's right. Guess which door it fits?'

Gail shook her head. 'I don't know. Please don't play any more games. I'm getting really worried now.'

'It's a key to Number 22.'

'But I've got my own!'

'You have Clive's key. This one is your own. I bumped into Clive soon after our chat and he said he was thinking of selling. So I made him an offer he couldn't refuse. This is your place, Gail. I've put your name on the deeds. It's my way of saying thank you for the Udagawa deal.'

'Really?' whispered Gail.

Paul held his breath. Had he done the right thing?

'That's the most wonderful gift you could ever have given me.' She flung her arms around his neck. 'How can I ever thank you?'

Paul's breath caught in his throat as he felt her soft cheek against his. 'Your face is reward enough.'

Then Gail's eyes filled with tears. 'If only Dad was here to see this.'

'He will be soon,' Paul assured her. That was the next challenge. But he couldn't tell Gail that, just in case it didn't work out. It had been a stroke of luck that Rob had rung the office phone when Gail had been out yesterday. Hopefully, he might just have changed his father-in-law's mind. Then again, you never knew with that man …

***

Wasn't it amazing how fast life could change in a few days let alone a few weeks! Things were really looking up all round – especially for Gail. And that's what mattered.

'When you told me how much my little girl was missing me, I had to come back,' Rob had said. 'Thanks, mate.'

Paul had given him a stern talking to then. 'Just don't do it again. You've no idea how upset she was.'

Of course he kept this quiet from Gail. All she knew

was that Rob had come back because he didn't like being away from her and that Paul had given him his room back at the hotel. Good old Dad had also played his part by buying a workshop and giving Rob a job. After all these chances, Paul told himself, his father-in-law had better not upset Gail again.

Then came some more good news. 'Guess what?' he said to Gail when he came back one evening to find her already there, cooking tea. (Smelt delicious!) 'Rosemary wants you to become assistant manager!'

'That's brilliant news!'

Everything was looking up. Maybe that's why he should have been prepared for it all going wrong again – but not in a way he'd imagined.

***

Gail was in his office when the phone rang. They were just about to leave for an early lunch – as he kept reminding her, they deserved a few treats and besides Gail wanted to show him some material she'd found for some new curtains. Now they were going to stay at Number 22 she wanted to put her own stamp on it.

'Go on – answer it,' said Gail. 'But please don't be too long.'

'I can't.'

'Why not?'

Paul felt slightly embarrassed. 'I'm the manager. It doesn't look good if I answer my own line.'

'But you've done it before!'

'Only after Jane has put it through.' Jane had popped out of the office on an errand.

'Oh for heaven's sake!' Laughing, she pretended to

dance round to the other side. 'I'll be your assistant then. 'Hello? This is Paul Robinson's phone.'

Then her face changed. For a minute, Paul thought it was Rob with another drama. 'Glen! Glen Matheson! How lovely to hear from you.'

Talk about a voice from the past. Glen had worked with them both at the airline.

'Can you pass him over?' mouthed Paul.

Gail shook her head. 'Your call came through to Paul's phone. Can you hang on for a minute?'

Then she cupped her hands over the phone. 'Sorry, Paul. It's me he wants to speak to. Mind if we do the curtains another day?'

'Sure.' It was clear she wanted him out of his own office. This didn't feel right. Paul had an uneasy feeling which lasted all day. And it didn't get any better when they drove home together.

'Glen's asked me out to dinner tonight. Isn't that exciting!'

Paul kept his eyes steadily on the road although he could sense his wife's excitement bubbling out.

'Do you know that it's been four years since I last saw him?'

'Really.' His hands tightened on the wheel.

'To be honest, I was attracted to him way back. In fact, if I hadn't met Jeremy, maybe we would have got together.'

'So he liked you too?'

Gail giggled. 'Didn't you notice? Everyone else on the staff kept saying what a good couple we'd make.'

Now he thought about it, there had been some gossip.

'Mind if we stop at the mall?'

'You want to look at the curtains after all?'

'No! I thought I might nip in and get a new dress. Maybe have my hair done. I've just about got time. Just here would be great. Thanks. Don't worry about picking me up. I'll get a cab back.'

At last he was able to stop the car and look at her face.

'You don't mind, do you?' she added.

'Of course not.' Paul felt his fingers biting into the palms of his hands. This was silly. She was entitled to go on dates just as he was. Not that his own romantic life amounted to much. He could have had a chance with Crystal – she'd rung him enough times since their last meeting – but there was no real spark as far as he was concerned.

'Just make sure you don't do anything that might embarrass us.' He gave a little laugh. 'You are married, remember?'

'Of course.' Her face was serious for a minute. 'Despite everything I've just said, Glen and I are just good mates. You know that, don't you?'

'I hope so,' Paul found himself thinking as he drove off. 'I really do.'

***

3.20 a.m! Still Paul couldn't sleep properly. All night, he'd been drifting off and then waking with a start, wondering if he could hear Gail coming back or whether she'd returned already. Should he knock on her door to check she was all right?

His mind went back to last night when Glen had turned up at the door of Number 22 to collect Gail. The man had looked so smooth and good-looking in his pilot's uniform, damn him! In fact, the more he thought about it, the more Paul remembered how he'd always thought Glen was a bit full of himself. How could someone like Gail go for a man like that?

Despite her assertion earlier that he was just an 'old mate', Paul could sense from Gail's excited face and vivacious manner that she liked him. She'd really looked beautiful in that blue dress which suited her so well. If only it could be him taking her out instead.

Hang on. What was he thinking of? Hadn't he offered her a divorce not that long ago? Yet hadn't he also been incredibly relieved when she'd turned it down?

'Sometimes,' Paul told himself firmly, 'you're behaving like a teenager who doesn't know what he wants.' Right. He'd knock on her door then.

No reply.

'Gail?' he whispered.

Still no reply. Feeling really awkward, he opened the door a crack. Gail's bed was smooth – and empty. Her work clothes were on the floor as if she'd been in a rush to dress. Gail was normally so tidy!

Wait? Was that the front door? Yes. Quickly, Paul shot back into his bedroom. Were those one set of footsteps or two coming up the stairs? Ruffling his hair to make it look like he'd just woken up, Paul went back out onto the landing.

'Hi!' Gail's lipstick was smudged. Had she just wiped her mouth with her hand by mistake or had someone been kissing her? Her eyes were bright and her speech very slightly slurred as if she'd had a tiny bit too much to drink. She was carrying her evening shoes in her hands. 'I tried not to wake you. So sorry.'

'That's fine.' Paul did his best to sound casual. 'Did

you enjoy yourself?'

'Brilliant! We went to a dinner dance and then a show and we chatted for ages about the old days and … But you don't want to know about all that, especially at this time of night. Let's catch up in the morning.'

Then she touched his shoulder. Every bone in his body tingled. 'Were you okay?'

'Course I was. Why wouldn't I be?'

His voice came out harder than he'd meant. Her eyes flickered. 'Good. That's all right then.'

Turning, she went into her room.

Paul stared at the door. Talk about being so near and yet so far. All it would take was for him to knock on it and say … Say what? He didn't even know himself.

No, he told himself, moving back across the landing to his own door. If Gail wanted some romance in her life, he would have to accept it. Just as long as no one got hurt.

Or was it too late already?

Twenty

GAIL

Concentrate, Gail told herself as she read through the latest batch of office memos. It was no good. All she could think of was how much she had enjoyed herself with Glen the other evening. She hadn't laughed so much for ages. Of course, it was awkward, pretending that she was happily married. At one point, it was almost on the tip of Gail's tongue to admit the truth … Luckily, she managed to stop herself in time.

'Can I come in?'

The knock on the door and the voice virtually came at the same time. 'Glen!' she said, feeling a lightness spreading right through her body. 'How great to see you. In fact, I've just been …'

She stopped.

'Thinking of me?' prompted Glen.

Quickly Gail composed herself. 'I was going to say that I've just been working really hard and could do with a quick break.'

'Glad I've come at the right time then.' He sat on the edge of Gail's desk so they were almost, but not quite touching. 'Hope you don't mind me just popping in but I'm in town for the weekend and bumped into a friend who has this great place in the country. I wondered if you and Paul would like to come up with me for a hack through the woods.'

'That would be amazing! I've always loved horses.'

'I remember you saying. What about Paul?'

'What about him?'

Gail jumped. She hadn't seen her husband coming in. Briefly she repeated Glen's invitation. 'But you don't really ride, do you, Paul? At least, not that well. So I'll just come up on my own.'

Glen raised his eyebrows. 'Do you mind, mate?'

'Not at all.'

Gail pretended to ignore the cool tone in Paul's voice. They had an arrangement, didn't they? Of course she would be careful but at the same time, there was something about Glen which was making her walk with a definite spring in her step. She also felt pretty fed up with Paul. He was always so hard-headed and emotionless – not just in business but in his private life. Quite clearly, he didn't care for her at all …

***

'How do I look?'

Gail gave a little twirl in her jodhpurs. Luckily, she'd managed to find them at the back of the wardrobe and they fitted as neatly as they'd done when she'd first had them.

'Very nice.'

Since Glen's invitation in the office, Paul had barely been speaking more than two words to her.

'They bring back memories.' She smoothed down the sides. 'Jeremy used to ride, you know.'

Paul shrugged. 'Sorry I don't match up.'

'Don't be silly! We all have our different interests in life, don't we?'

'Sounds as though one of yours has just arrived. Isn't that Glen's car outside?'

Gail reached the door before Paul had another go at spoiling her day. 'Hi!'

'Wow.' Glen gazed down on her. 'You look amazing. Doesn't she, Paul? You're a lucky man, I must say. Sure you don't mind me whisking your wife off for the day?'

'Why should I?'

How childish! Gail deliberately laughed out loud. 'See you later, darling!'

For a minute, as Glen opened the car door for her (such a gentleman) she felt a brief flash of worry. Had she been a bit mean to Paul back then? After all, she had to admit he'd been very generous over giving her the house. Then again, she'd worked for that deal. And it wasn't as though she'd made a fuss about Paul going out with Crystal. It works both ways!

***

'This is lovely,' breathed Gail as she and Glen trotted side by side through the green leafy woods. Her mare was the perfect height at 15.5 hands and so well behaved. She certainly lived up to her name 'Serenity'.

'Looks like our horses have the hots for each other,' joked Glen as his bay gelding – a 16 plus hands steed called Viking – stopped to nuzzle hers.

'Good taste,' quipped Gail, tugging at the reins. 'Come on, Serenity. Never trust a man when he says he loves you.'

'Do you mean that?' Glen turned serious for minute.

'No – of course not.' Be careful, Gail told herself. But at the same time she couldn't help feeling cross with Paul for being so moody. 'I can't remember the last time I had so much fun – apart from our night out at the club of course.'

'Yeah?' Glen was frowning. 'What about your honeymoon?'

'Actually,' she replied lightly, 'we didn't have one. Work has been so busy that we haven't had time.' Then, before her companion could ask any more awkward questions, she cantered on ahead.

All too soon, or so it seemed, they were back in Ramsay Street. 'Thanks so much,' said Gail as they turned into the road and stopped, waiting for a parking space. 'I've had a great day.'

'Really?' Glen raised an eyebrow. 'I reckon you're only here to wind up Paul. It seems to me that you two have got a bit of friction going on there.'

'Nonsense,' retorted Gail. 'He's just a bit tied up with his work at the moment. Actually, we understand each other very well. Neither of us are the jealous type. He is very happy for me to have my friends and I'm happy for him to have his.'

As if to prove the point she leaned across and gave Glen a kiss on his cheek. But as she did so, he moved his face and her lips came perilously close to his mouth.

'Sorry,' she said embarrassed.

'Don't be,' he murmured. 'That was an unexpected bonus to a perfect day.'

***

Later, still excited about the hack and – truth be told, Glen's obvious admiration – Gail nipped round to Number 26 for a quick chat. 'How did your riding go?' asked Helen, putting on the kettle.

Gail felt herself flushing. 'Great. I'd forgotten how much I'd missed the thrill. It felt so natural being back in the saddle again.'

'Is that so?'

'Why do you say it like that?'

They were sitting at the kitchen table now, having a mug of coffee. 'Look, love.' Helen reached out, running her finger meaningfully over Gail's wedding ring. 'I don't want to interfere in your marriage but I saw you in the car earlier with Glen. You were kissing …'

If only she could sink right into the floor! Gail took a deep gulp. 'It was just a quick brush on the cheek to say thank you for today. It didn't mean any more than that.'

But Helen's face clearly showed she wasn't convinced. 'I have to ask you, Gail. I don't need to ask Paul about his feelings because I know him well enough to tell they are true. But do you really love my grandson?'

'Yes.' Gail could feel her face growing even redder. 'I really do.'

'Then I'm sorry for asking. Like I said, I know Paul worships the ground you tread on. I hope you feel the same way. He went through enough with Terry, bless her soul. I wouldn't want to see him hurt again.'

'Nor me.'

Helen patted her hand. 'Then that's all right. You'll have to forgive me but as the matriarchal head of this family, I like to make sure that everything is running smoothly.' Her face hardened. 'Because if it doesn't, they have me to reckon with.'

***

Paul continued to be a bit quiet for the next few days. Perhaps it was just as well he wasn't around to hear the phone calls that Glen kept making, inviting her on more dates. 'I'm sorry,' Gail said every time, 'but I'm snowed under with work.'

It was true but part of her didn't want to upset Paul. The other part was desperate to accept Glen's invitations and go back to having fun instead of playing this let's-pretend-we're-married game which at times seemed to make perfect sense and at other times appeared downright stupid.

Then came the call from Rosemary ...

'You'll never believe it,' said Gail as soon as she got home that night.

Paul was lying on the sofa, watching television. The lounge room was a mess with his jacket lying on the chair and muddy footprints on the carpet. How often had she told him to take off his shoes! If it wasn't for the news she had to give him, she'd make a fuss right now.

'I had a call from Rosemary. She's asked me to go over to America to help with the project she's working on. It's very last-minute but it sounds really exciting.'

Paul reached for the remote control and switched channels to a comedy programme without saying anything.

'I don't have to go if you don't want me to.'

'I don't mind at all.' Paul's tone was as cold as it had been since Glen had come back into her life.

He hadn't even asked her how long she'd be gone for – or when she was going!

'I'll only be away for two weeks.'

'Fine.'

Canned laughter rang out from the TV set.

'Okay then.' Gail turned away. 'I'll go and pack. I'm leaving tomorrow so I want to get myself sorted ...'

'Don't you want to eat first?'

'Actually, I've lost my appetite.'

'Suit yourself.'

This wasn't the Paul she knew and loved. Earlier, when Helen had asked if she really did love him, Gail had meant it when she replied in the affirmative. But you could love people in lots of different ways, couldn't you? It didn't have to be the romantic type. Besides, right now, he was behaving so badly that he wasn't particularly likeable. There was a big difference between that and lovable.

***

Later, when Gail was ironing a rather pretty blue dress for one of the smart business dinners that Rosemary had mentioned, she was conscious of Paul hovering at her side.

'How's it going?'

He sounded much nicer than earlier.

'I'm a bit nervous about going away on a trip,' she confided. 'Silly when you think of our days on the airline.'

'I suppose you've got out of the habit.'

'Exactly.'

'Careful. You'll scorch it.'

Whoops! Gail had almost forgotten to take the iron off.

'I'm going to struggle with work when you're away,' he continued. 'You're my right hand girl, as you know.'

He'd really changed his tune about her going!

'Would you like me to cancel it? I'm sure Rosemary would understand.'

'No. Don't do that. I wouldn't want to spoil your fun.'

'It's not pleasure you know. It's work.'

'Don't be so moody.'

'You're the one who's being moody. You've hardly spoken to me since I went riding with Glen.'

He mumbled something indistinct. It sounded like 'That's not surprising' but she couldn't be certain.

'Well, I'm sure he'll miss you.'

'So you won't?'

'I didn't say that.'

'I should think not. After all, you can always see Crystal while I'm away. Just make sure that Lucy doesn't spot you and get upset again.'

'That's not fair.'

'None of this is fair!' Switching off the iron, she picked up her dress. 'I'm very grateful for the house, Paul. But you can't buy me off. There are times when I wonder if we've dug ourselves into a hole with this arrangement. I know I said I wanted the companionship but maybe, on reflection, we've put ourselves into an impossible situation – both tied to each other without being honest to the rest of the world.'

'If that's how you feel, maybe you're better off going.'

'Fine.'

Gail flounced up to her bedroom.

***

When she came down the next morning, Paul had left for work. There wasn't even a note. At least she knew where she stood. But it was still hurtful.

Only ten minutes now until the taxi would be here. There was just time to make that call she'd been putting off. 'Glen? It's …'

'Gail!'

How lovely that he recognized her voice and that he seemed so delighted to hear her.

'I'm afraid I've to go away for a two week business trip to the States …'

He cut in before she could finish. 'That's a real shame. I was hoping to whisk you back off to the woods at the weekend for another hack.'

'I'd have liked that,' she replied wistfully.

'Make sure you call as soon as you come back. Okay? Wish I could be flying you. Then we'd have more time together.'

'Glen,' she said quietly, 'I think we both need to remember that I'm married.'

'Sure but like you said earlier when we were riding, there's nothing like old friends.'

'No but …' Gail's attention was suddenly drawn to the taxi which was pulling up outside. 'I've got to go now. See you soon.'

Glen showed more feeling than Paul! Was she making a big mistake here?

'Is this all?' asked the taxi driver as he carried her case out.

Years of flying had taught Gail to pack sensibly. 'Yes thanks.'

He shut the car door behind her. Just as they were about to move off, another car came round the corner. Paul! He'd come to say goodbye after all.

Quickly she wound down the window. 'I'm so glad you're here.'

His face was set as though she was a stranger. 'I only came back to give you these.' He handed her some papers through the car window. 'They're for Aunt Rosemary. Could you make sure she gets them, please?'

'Of course. See you when I get back then.'

'Sure.'

She put up the window.

As she did so, she saw his lips move. If she was a lip-reader – which she wasn't – she might think he was saying 'I love you'. Her heart began to beat faster.

'Sorry, I missed that,' she said winding down the window.

'I just told you to have a good time.'

'Right. Thanks.'

Gail pressed the window to go up again, leant back in her seat and felt her eyes fill with tears as the taxi drove off.

At the last moment, she looked back through the rear window. Paul was standing there, staring, as though he didn't want to let her out of his sight.

Twenty-one

PAUL

The last two weeks had seemed so long without Gail. Number 22 simply wasn't the same. Even though he'd wanted to move before because it was on the small side, their home seemed so empty without Gail's presence.

How he missed her laughter and all the other little things like her shoes by the front door or the way she laid the table for breakfast the night before or the radio which was always switched to her favourite station.

If only they hadn't ended on such a bad note. As soon as she was back, he'd put it right. He had to!

'You look happy,' said Helen when she saw him coming back with a large bunch of pink roses from the shops.

'I am! Gail's back today.'

'I know.' Helen touched his arm. 'We've all missed her.' Her eye fell on the beautiful blooms. 'I'm sure Gail will really appreciate those.'

'They're a …'

He'd been going to say 'make up present' but had managed to stop himself in time. 'They're a welcome home gift,' he said instead. 'Better get going. Thought I'd surprise her by meeting her at the airport.'

'I thought she'd booked a taxi.'

'She had – but I've cancelled it.'

'I see. Seems a bit odd you didn't sort all this out to begin with.'

'Look, Gran, like I said, I've really got to go.'

'Sure.' She gave him a hug. 'I don't want to get in the way of true love!'

Nor do I, thought Paul as he quickened his step. There'd been enough of that already.

***

There were so many people coming through the arrival gates that for a minute, Paul wondered if he might have missed her. But no. There was Gail, looking beautiful in her travelling black and white trousers and neat little jacket. She was looking round, clearly searching for the taxi placard but when she saw Paul, she seemed irritated rather than pleased.

Oh dear. He didn't have a good feeling about this.

He made to kiss her on the cheek but she moved her face away. 'I wasn't expecting you. What about the taxi?'

'Don't worry. I told them I was picking up my wife instead.'

Was it his imagination or did she flinch when he used the word 'wife'?

'I've missed you, Gail.' He tried to put an arm around

her shoulder but again she moved away. 'I thought we could use the time in the car on the way home to talk about a few things.'

'That's good.'

His heart leaped. 'Really?'

'There are a few things I need to talk to *you* about too.'

Her voice was heavy.

'That sounds a bit serious.' Paul tried to keep his voice steady.

'It is.'

They walked in silence weaving their way through the crowds towards his car but as soon as they got inside, Gail turned to him. 'The thing is, Paul, that I want a divorce after all. My time in the States has allowed me to think. I can't go on with our so-called marriage. We only did it to nail the deal and now it's done.'

What? 'But I thought you said you wanted the security of being in a family.'

'I do.' She made to touch his arm and then seemed to think better of it. 'And that's why I'm doing this.'

Paul's head was spinning. 'Did something happen in America to make you decide to do this?'

'Yes.'

He knew it! She'd fallen in love with someone – maybe Glen, damn him, had flown over to be with her.

'It was Rosemary.'

'You didn't tell her!'

'Of course not. But being with her every day and watching how she trusted me, made me realise that I can't live the rest of my life as a lie. Then there's everyone else. I love Helen as though she was my own gran, and Lucy is like a little sister.'

'But they'll all be so upset!'

Gail sighed. 'It will be worse if we go on. Look at the problems we had when Lucy thought you were cheating on me. This can't go on. We'll only be "caught out" again.'

Paul felt his hands sweating on the steering wheel. 'How are we going to tell them?'

'I don't know. Let's work it out when we get home.'

'And I can't make you change your mind?'

They were at traffic lights now so he could look across safely and see her face. She was shaking her head. 'I'm sorry, Paul. Trust me. This is hard for me too. But my mind is made up.'

***

Maybe, thought Paul, if he left Gail to herself for a few hours, she might have thought twice. When he came downstairs, he found her wandering wistfully around, touching the photograph frames of their wedding pictures on the mantelpiece. So he was right!

But when she saw him, she jumped as though she'd been caught doing something wrong. 'I was about to make tea,' she said in a distant off-hand manner. 'Do you want something?'

'No thanks.' He turned away. 'I'm not hungry.'

'Don't be like that.'

'Like what?'

'You know. Are you acting like this because I want a divorce?'

'What do *you* think? I've been snowed under with work while you've been away and now I have this to deal with.'

Gail shut the patio windows leading onto the barbie area. 'Shh. The neighbours will hear.'

'I don't care.'

'Then you should. You also ought to get your priorities right. All you care about is work. Isn't that why we got married in the first place?'

'Yes. No. I mean, I wouldn't have married anyone else.'

'Like Crystal, you mean?' She laughed. 'No one else would be crazy enough to go into a marriage of convenience like I did.'

Paul felt like tearing his hair out. 'Well now it's not so convenient, as you put it, maybe you're right. We'll go ahead with that divorce.'

'Good.'

He made for the stairs.

'Where are you going?' Gail's voice was sharp.

'To bed.'

'So early?'

'I'm not hungry. I don't want to go out. I'm not ready to face my family. And you clearly don't want me around. So it seems like the best thing to do.'

'Paul?'

'What?'

He turned, expecting to see anger on her face. Instead, she seemed all confused and vulnerable and upset. It was all he could do not to put his arms around her. 'Yes?' he said softly.

'You really don't want any tea?'

Was it his imagination or had she been going to say something else and chickened out.

'No thank you.'

'Suit yourself.' She turned on her heels, and went into the kitchen.

He'd been wrong. Gail obviously didn't want him around. The sooner he was out of here, the better as far as she was concerned. Paul went into his room and sat on the edge of his bed trying to work out the practicalities. At some point he'd have to tell Gran, although he'd ask Gail first not to reveal that they'd only married for business reasons. Something told him that Gran would see through that anyway. She was one of the few people who had always understood him. She'd know that Paul had feelings for Gail; feelings which he could barely admit to himself in case everything went wrong again. Just as it had with Terry.

But what if he took the plunge and came clean with his wife?

No. That wouldn't work. 'Be honest,' Paul told himself as he tossed and turned all night. 'You've just got to accept it. Gail doesn't love you back.'

Then again, what if he made one last attempt?

***

Paul woke early with a start the next morning as all the events of yesterday came flooding back. There were movements downstairs, indicating that Gail was already up in the kitchen. Better be quick in case she went out somewhere.

Pulling on his dressing gown, Paul almost ran down the stairs. A lovely smell of coffee was filtering out and the smell of freshly baked bread. 'Look,' he said, charging into the kitchen before he lost his nerve. 'I don't want a divorce. I love you. And you know what, Gail? I think you love me too. In fact …'

He forced himself then to look up and face her. But there was no one there. Only then did he notice that the door was open.

'Hi.' Gail was coming back in with a dried-up looking plant. 'Did you say something to me? I couldn't hear out there.'

'No. Yes. I mean, it doesn't matter.'

Gail looked down at the pot plant. 'You were meant to have watered this when I was away.'

'Sorry. One more thing I can't get right, then.'

'Jeremy gave this to me soon after we were married.'

'Given his behaviour, I wouldn't think that the plant could mean so much.'

'Well it does.'

What was the point? Gail was a mass of contradictions. He just couldn't win.

'See you later. I'm going out for the day.'

'In your dressing gown?'

He'd almost forgotten about that. A few weeks ago, they might have laughed. But now it was all dead serious.

'After I've got ready. See you later.'

***

Paul spent the whole day sitting by the lake at Lassiters, watching other couples go by along with families with prams and strollers. What would life have been like if Terry had lived? Could he have forgiven her after everything she had done? Had he been right to shop her to the police? And now he'd messed up his life all over again.

'Why don't you be honest,' Paul told himself. 'Suggesting marriage was a convenience at the time but didn't part of you secretly want to marry Gail – even though you might not have admitted it to yourself?'

Eventually he got up. No good crying about the past. He had to go forwards. Whether he liked it or not.

In a way, he was surprised to find Gail at home when he returned. 'Not out riding with Glen then?'

She gave him a withering look. 'No. And whatever you think, he's not why I want to end our sham of a marriage.'

'Whatever you say.' Oh dear. He hadn't wanted it to be so confrontational. 'Listen,' he continued. 'I've decided. If you want, I'll move back to Lassiters. You stay here – it's yours anyway.'

'Okay. Thanks.' There was a decided note of relief in her voice. 'Would you like me to resign from my job?'

'No.' His answer came out fast. 'We work well together.'

'Yes. We do.' Now she sounded almost regretful.

He hesitated. 'And there isn't someone else … in America?'

Her words now whipped out angrily. 'Of course not.'

'But why do you suddenly want a divorce now? After I'd offered it to you before.'

'And I told you! It was being with Rosemary. I realised I can't turn my emotions on and off like a tap, like some people can.'

'Meaning me?'

'Yes.'

Talk about pot calling the kettle black. 'But that's what *you* do!'

'No I don't.' Gail had her head in her hands. 'Look, I know what happened with Terry has made you scared to show your feelings.'

'You don't know anything about that time. You weren't there!'

'And you don't understand the pain I went through with Jeremy.'

'Then we really have had it, haven't we?'

Gail nodded sadly. 'It looks like it.'

Right. Then in that case, Paul told himself, there was one person he had to tell before any of the others.

***

'I don't get it.' Shock was written all over his father's face at the workshop. (Luckily no one else was there at the time.) 'I thought you and Gail got hitched rather quickly, to be honest, but at your age, I assumed you knew what you were doing. So why are you both having doubts, as you put it?'

Paul shrugged. 'We just are.'

If only he could tell him the whole story. But then everyone would think even worse of him. Getting married for the sake of a business deal? Even though it had seemed to make sense at the time, Paul began to wonder what on earth he'd been thinking of.

'Please don't say anything to anyone else yet,' he pleaded. 'Not even Gail.'

'Okay.' Jim seemed uncertain. He clapped him on the back. 'I'm here, if you ever need me. You know that.'

The following day, Jim knocked on the door. Luckily Gail had gone 'shopping' but Paul wouldn't have put it past her to be with Glen.

'Look, there's something that doesn't seem right. No. Don't try and make excuses. You're my son and I know you. I'm not going to tell your gran about the two of you until you tell me what's really going on.'

Paul groaned. 'It's not easy.'

'I can guess. It's Glen, isn't it? I thought from the way that Gail was talking about that ride in the woods that she liked that man a bit more than she should have done. But that doesn't mean you give up just like that!'

Jim put a hand on each of his shoulders, forcing him to look straight back. 'You can't just roll over and let her go.'

'It's not like that!' Paul felt his words come out in an anguished cry. 'There are things you don't know.'

'Then why don't you tell me, son. I'm listening.'

Twenty-Two

GAIL

'Are you busy?'

No need to look up to see who was speaking! Just because Paul was her boss, thought Gail, didn't mean he could just interrupt her work like this. Maybe he'd hoped to catch her on the phone to Glen. The truth was that she'd been in two minds about picking up the receiver and telling her old friend all about it.

'Yes,' she said shortly, signing the document in front of her. 'I *am* busy.'

'Gail, please.'

He was standing next to her now. She could almost feel the heat of his body.

'Will you come out with me tonight? No strings attached. I'm not going to try and talk you out of your decision – I just want to talk and I think it will help if we did that outside the house.'

'No.'

The word snapped out of her mouth. Maybe it was

because she was angry with herself, Gail thought, for agreeing to such a crazy marriage set up. In the last few days, she'd been doing a lot of thinking. It was clear to her now that Paul had taken advantage of her. She'd been so shocked after Jeremy's accident that she'd have agreed to almost anything. Well, now she was stronger and able to make better decisions.

Gail stood up and moved away from Paul so she was on the other side of the desk. 'In fact, I've been writing my resignation letter. Here it is.'

'What?' The shock on Paul's face was almost gratifying. 'Why? We've had a good day together. That meeting this morning went well. We can still work as a team. And …'

'Stop. Please. Right there.' Gail felt tears pricking her eyes. 'I just can't bear you any more.'

Where did those words come from? She hadn't meant to go that far. Or had she?

Instantly, Paul's eyes went cold. His expression froze. It was as though the light had gone out of his body. 'I see,' he said, taking the letter. 'Well, you'd better leave now then.'

Gail hadn't been expecting that. 'In front of the others? What will everyone say?'

'I don't care. Leave your stuff. I'll arrange for it to be picked up later. And don't expect me back at the house anytime soon.'

***

If she had any doubts before, Gail told herself, they were gone now. Paul was a … well, words weren't enough to describe what he was. And if that was him at the door right now – knocking as though he'd forgotten his key – she'd give him a piece of her mind.

'Glen!'

'Hi! Would you believe it if I said I was in the area and couldn't resist dropping by to say hello to my favourite friend ... Wait! What's wrong.'

Glen took both her hands and drew her to him in a hug. 'You've been crying.'

'It's ... it's Paul.'

Alarm swept his face. 'He's not been hurt, has he?'

'NO.' Gail's voice came out in a gigantic sob. 'It's *me* he's been hurting. That man is unfeeling and heartless and ... and impossible.'

Glen was leading her towards the sofa. How often had she imagined this in her head? But now it was happening, it didn't feel right. Why, after everything, did she wish it was Paul who was doing this?

'Look,' he said, gently pulling her down next to him. 'I don't know what's been happening but it's plain to see that you are very much in love with your husband.'

What was he saying? This was Glen's cue to tell her how much *he* loved her!

'Don't be ridiculous. I ...'

'No. Listen to me Gail. I've seen you look at him. There's something there which you never had with Jeremy and which I wish might have existed between us in another life. But this is the here and now. Like I said, I don't understand what's brought this on, but I do know something. You two are right for each other.'

Gail jumped up. 'How do you know? Anyway, it's none of your business. You don't know the whole story.'

'Then tell me.'

Gail hesitated. 'I can't. It's too complicated and … and private … Anyway I know my own mind. And divorcing Paul is the best decision I've made in a long time. I *will* tell you everything but it's not right until the immediate family know first.'

He made a 'fair enough' gesture. 'Would it help if I talked to Paul? You know, be a sort of go between?'

'No.' Suddenly Gail didn't want to see Glen any more than she'd wanted to see Paul earlier. 'If you really want to help, please just go. I've got an important call to make.'

Glen looked crestfallen. 'If that's what you want.' He took her hand. 'But if there's anything I can do – anything – give me a ring.'

'Thanks.' Gail almost shook him off. 'Do you mind if you see yourself out?'

As soon as the door was closed, she picked up the phone, mentally working out the time in the States.

'Rosemary? This is Gail. I'm sorry to bother you but something's happened. No. It's not Paul. Well, it is, but he's all right.'

Gail took a deep breath, struggling to maintain a professional composure. 'I'm afraid things aren't good between us at the moment and … well, I've decided to quit. Yes. That's right. I'm talking about both my marriage and my job.'

***

Paul didn't come back that night. Where was he? Had he done something stupid? Should she call his family? Or the police even? Then again, he'd probably gone to Crystal. That would be it. He'd be telling her right now that his wife had never understood him and that tart would be comforting him, whispering that she'd always liked him …

By the time she woke up in the morning, Gail knew exactly what to do. With any luck, she told herself, walking into the Daniels Corporation offices, this was the last time she'd ever need to come here again.

'Good morning,' she said briskly, taking in Paul's dishevelled appearance. Her eyes fell on a duvet on the reception sofa. So he'd spent the night *here*?

'Morning,' he said coolly. 'I didn't expect to see you here.'

'As you didn't come back last night, I thought I'd give you my news here instead.'

His face tensed. 'What news?'

'Rosemary has offered me a job as her executive assistant, over in New York. She says she values me – which is more than you do otherwise you wouldn't have tried to buy me off for the Japanese deal.'

'I didn't try to "buy you off" as you put it. You could have said no.'

Maybe. But it seemed too late to take her words back.

'Well congratulations anyway,' added Paul, scathingly. 'You've finally got what you wanted all along. The perfect career without a man to get in your way. I wish you every success.'

'That's not fair!'

'Are you sure? You've always been ambitious, Gail! When Jeremy was alive you liked being the wife of a famous racing driver. And despite you acting as though our marriage was all *my* fault, you went along with it – even declaring that you didn't want out when I suggested it weeks ago.'

I'm confused, Gail wanted to say. One minute I want you and the next I don't. Help me by saying that you love me too.

Hopefully, she waited as if a miracle might happen. Then she saw it. Right on his desk in front of her nose. His diary.

'Go on then,' taunted Paul as she picked it up. 'Throw something at me if you want.'

'No,' she said slowly. 'I just wanted to check the writing. *Crystal. 1 o'clock*. You don't hang around, do you?'

'You've got it wrong.'

'I don't think so.' Gail burst into tears. 'But at least I know for sure now that I'm making the right decision. Goodbye, Paul.'

Then rushing past Jane who was doubtless coming in to see what all the noise was about, she ran out of the building and into her car. Only then, with the doors closed, did Gail put her head on the wheel and weep as though her heart was going to break.

Twenty-three

PAUL

Work. It was the only thing that kept him sane when terrible things happened. Hadn't Paul learned that after Terry had died? In a way, Gail's leaving was like a death too. A slow extended one as the date for her departure approached.

Of course everyone in the office knew something was up after Gail had left so suddenly the other day, though he obviously hadn't gone into details.

'Gail's resigned,' he'd told Jane abruptly.

'No! Why?'

'She's going to work for Rosemary in New York.' He'd turned away so she couldn't see the anguish on his face. Then he braced himself to turn back again. 'It's a great opportunity for her and we both felt she shouldn't turn it down.'

'Sure.' Jane was clearly uncertain.

'I'd like you to fill in until I find her replacement.'

That should please her. Jane was a bright girl and was,

he knew, keen to advance her own career.

'Wow. Thanks. But is there any chance that Gail might come back in a few months?'

'I don't think so,' said Paul slowly.

'I see.' She'd got it now. 'I'm really sorry. Please, Paul, let me know if there is anything I can do.'

Sympathy was the last thing he needed! 'There is, actually. I'd like to talk through the paperwork for the Japanese deal. In fact, let's start right now. There's a lot to be done and I want to get back early to help Gail with her packing.'

***

GAIL

Nearly finished. Gail looked around at the suitcases which she'd packed neatly with most of her clothes. How often had she done this? Too many times! All she'd ever wanted in life was security, a man who loved her, a career and maybe children one day. So how come she found herself here – changing life paths all over again?

Was she really doing the right thing? The last few days had been even more awkward than normal, especially as she still wasn't sure whether to believe Paul's 'excuse' about the 1 p.m. date in his diary. 'I promise,' he'd said. 'I only wrote that down because Crystal had said she wanted me to meet her the other day. But then I rang and said I couldn't.'

'Why?'

'What does it matter to you? We're free agents. Hadn't we said that at the beginning?'

Yes. He was right. After that, she'd tried to be fair,

telling Paul that he was welcome to live in the house as she probably wouldn't be coming back again.

And now here he was – even though he said he'd be spending all day in the office.

'Hi. Thought I'd give you a hand.' He looked around at all the cases. 'So you really are going for good.'

'I did tell you that.'

'Yes, but we've said quite a few things in the past that we've both taken back, haven't we?'

'Not this time.'

He shrugged, picking up a case. 'This is heavy.'

'I'm sorry.'

'No problem. I can manage.'

'No. I mean I'm … well, I'm sorry for everything.'

'Please don't, Gail.' He turned his back on her but she could hear his words clearly enough. 'I've had enough of these mixed messages.'

'Well at least I show my feelings.'

'What was that?'

'Nothing.'

'Thank goodness! You're still here!'

It was Helen. 'Jim told me you were going today.'

'What else did he tell you?' asked Paul quickly.

'Nothing. Only that he's very upset – like all of us. And what about your father, Gail?'

She felt a stab of guilt. 'I feel bad about leaving him but I'm going to fly him over for Christmas to see me.'

'Look, love.' Helen took her by the hand and then reached out for Paul with the other. 'Will you let me mediate for you, to try and save your marriage? I've had a lot of experience in life. Talking to me might help and I promise that I won't be judgemental in any way.'

'Neither of us have cheated on the other, if that's what you're implying,' said Gail quickly.

'I'm not saying you have but it's so quick. First your marriage itself and now the break up. I just want to help you both see sense.'

'I know you mean well but there's nothing that can be done. Is there, Paul?'

He shook his head. 'I'm afraid not.' His face was blank. Didn't the man have any emotion?

'But you will come and say goodbye to all the family, won't you?' Helen's eyes were full of tears.

'Of course.' Gail felt her own eyes prick too.

As soon as Helen had gone, Gail rounded on Paul. 'You've got to tell her the truth! It's not fair. She thinks that one of us has been having an affair. I know it. If you don't tell her, then I will.'

Paul shrugged as he took the last suitcase to the door. 'You know what, Gail? You can do what you like. You usually do.'

That wasn't fair! Was it?

Gail checked the last of her wardrobes. They looked so strange being empty.

'If you want to see the family, we'd better go now.' Paul was back.

Gail braced herself. This was going to be tough. Not only did she have to say goodbye but she was also about to destroy their faith in her.

'Scott!' she heard Paul say.

Word had clearly got around.

'I can't believe you're going, Gail!' Her brother-in-law drew her to him in a big hug. 'We're going to miss you so much. It won't be the same without you.'

Gail never thought she'd feel this much pain again after Jeremy's cheating and then his death. But now her chest was hurting so much that she could barely speak. 'I'm sorry too.'

Scott looked confused. 'I don't get it. What went wrong?'

'Nothing.' Paul's voice cut in. 'Gail got offered this great job with Rosemary and well, we just need some time apart. It's worked out quite well, actually.'

Yes. Sure, thought Gail bitterly. 'Actually,' she said, 'we're on our way to your place now. Why don't you come with us? And Paul, take that document with you, will you?' She glanced across at the piece of paper on the coffee table, giving him a meaningful look. 'We need to make everything perfectly clear.'

***

PAUL

This was awful, thought Paul, as Gran ushered them in. In some ways, he just wished Gail could get on that plane so all this would be over with. What was Gran going to think of him?

'I need to talk to you both,' Helen said.

'We've been through this before, Gran. There's nothing to be said.'

'I can't believe that.'

Gail cut in. 'Go on, Paul. Show her.'

There was no option. Reluctantly, Paul handed over the document.

'What's this?' Her eyes widened. 'A pre-nup agreement?'

'Just read it. Please,' said Gail tearfully.

They both watched as she did so. Her jaw virtually dropped. 'I don't believe it. You're saying you got married for business reasons just so you could secure the Japanese deal? So ... so you weren't really in love?'

'It seemed the right thing to do at the time,' Paul said firmly. 'Mr Udagawa was so keen on family values. You remember. He wanted to give his business to a family man.'

Helen shook her head. 'I thought I brought you up to be honest.' Then she turned to Gail. 'And I'm surprised you went along with it. Then again, you were probably still in shock after Jeremy.'

She took another look at the document as if the wording might have changed in the last few seconds. 'And now the deal's in the bag, you're off. Just like that. I have to say, I thought you both had more integrity than this.'

Tears were streaming down Gail's face now. 'You're right. I was stupid. But I have to say that I really do love you all. That's why I've ended this charade of a marriage. I'm going so that Paul and I can make a new start. An honest one. Goodbye, Helen.'

He watched as his wife embraced his gran. 'I hope I'll see you again one day.'

***

Gran would hardly speak to him after that. And no wonder! There were still a few hours before the taxi came to collect Gail. There was only one place to seek refuge. Back to his desk at the Daniels Corporation.

'Paul!'

Scott again! Why did everyone feel they had the right

to barge into his life, let alone his office?

'Look. Gran's told me everything. Okay. It was a bit weird when I heard the truth but it doesn't matter why you got married – the thing is that you two really love each other. Go on. Admit it.'

What was the point in denying it any more? Gail was going, wasn't she? 'Okay. But what can I do about it? I don't want to get hurt again after Terry and anyway, Gail's mind is set. She's off. It's probably for the best.'

'But she loves you too!'

'Then why is she going?'

'For the same reasons as you! Don't you see? She doesn't want to get hurt again either. Honestly, mate, you're making a huge mistake if you let her go without putting up a fight.'

How could he explain? 'I've tried.'

'Then you'll just have to try a bit harder. Or maybe I will.'

'If you're talking about being some kind of mediator, forget it. Gran's had a shot and it's no good.'

Scott was already at the door. 'Let's just see, shall we?'

***

GAIL

Scott again?

'It's okay. Gran's told me everything and I get it. I really do.' He looked around, taking in the cases. 'Why don't you cancel that taxi and let me take you to the airport?'

She felt a flood of relief. At least she hadn't lost her

little brother-in-law then. 'That would be great. Thanks.'

'You know,' he said, picking up a bag, 'Paul loves you. He told me.'

Gail stopped still, her breath catching in her throat. 'I don't believe it.'

'It's true.'

'Then he should tell me himself.'

'Just what I said. But you know my brother. Keeps his cards close to his chest after what happened last time.'

'And that's exactly why I'm not holding my breath.'

'All I'm saying is think about it. This one ready?'

He gestured to a second bag.

'Yes. Thanks.'

As he carried it out of the room, Gail began to sob. Had Paul really meant it when he told his brother he loved her? Or was he just trying to make out that she was the bad guy in all this?

'You're leaving that one then?' asked Scott as he returned.

Gail glanced at the box and nodded. Then, when his back was turned, she reached out and took the photograph that was sticking out of it. It was one of the wedding pictures: her favourite! She and Paul looked so happy, as if they were really in love. Swiftly she put it in her handbag.

As she got into the car, Gail took one last look back at her home, Ramsay Street and Number 26. Her eyes blurred and her chest tightened. To think this was the last time she would ever see this place again. After this, there could be no going back.

'Where are we going?' she asked as he took a right and then a left. 'This isn't the route to the airport.'

Scott glanced across at her from the driving seat. 'Thought we'd pop into The Waterhole on the way. We've got plenty of time. The family's all there to say goodbye to you properly.'

Gail felt her fingers biting into her palm. 'I can't. I'm embarrassed and ashamed.'

'Then you'll have to get a taxi after all.'

'But I cancelled the first! It might take a while to get another.'

'Sorry, Gail. That's the choice. It's up to you.'

He'd set her up! But it looked as though there was no getting out of it …

***

'Gail, love.' Helen's arms were around her. 'I couldn't let you go without saying goodbye properly and making up.'

It was so lovely to hug this woman who had become part of her life. 'I don't know what to say, Helen. I'm so very sorry. Please believe me when I say that my feelings for you all have been genuine.'

'We know that, dear.'

Hugging Helen again, Gail saw Paul coming out of the bar. As her husband's face met hers, he quickly turned round again. That proved it! He didn't love her at all.

'Leave him, please!' she called out as Scott followed him.

'What's going on?' asked Gran.

Words like 'face up' and 'you're going to lose her' came drifting out from the buzz of conversation at the bar. Then Paul disappeared completely. She shouldn't have come here!

'I need to ring for a taxi,' she said quickly.

'I thought Scott was taking you.'

'No. I need to go now.'

She had to get outside – quickly – before the tears started. Finding a quiet corner, Gail sobbed and sobbed. How could Paul be so unkind? And how could she have allowed herself to get into this mess? Then she felt a hand on her shoulder. She knew that touch!

'Gail?' It was Paul's voice.

'Please. Just go away.'

'But I can't. Listen to me. Just for a minute.'

Gail wanted to run but her legs wouldn't move.

'My little brother's right.' There was a wobble in his voice. 'I'm not scared of taking risks in business. In fact, I see them as a challenge. But, well, when it comes to love, it's different. I'm scared. And I think you are too.'

The tears were coming faster now. Gail could only nod. She'd never heard Paul sound so gentle before.

'You see, I love you.'

Had she heard him right?

'Say that again,' she sniffed, wiping her eyes with her hand and, in so doing, smudging her lipstick. What did she look like now?

'I love you,' he repeated.

'Then why didn't you say so before?'

'I told you. I'm scared.' He cupped her face between his hands. 'I should have told you before. But now I need to know how you feel.'

'I love you too, you silly thing.'

They both burst out laughing and crying at the same time.

'I thought it was Glen you cared for.' Paul flexed his arm muscles in a jokey way. 'In fact, I was getting ready to challenge him to a fight!'

'You're not the fighting type,' she teased.

His face turned more serious. 'No, but I should have been. Then I might have fought harder for you and we wouldn't be in this mess.' He glanced at his watch. 'You'll have to go now if you're going to get that plane.'

'Do you want me to?'

They were even closer now.

'No. Of course not. What about you?'

'What will Rosemary think?'

Paul was holding her now. 'She'll be highly relieved that we've both seen sense.'

'Go on, mate! Kiss her!'

Both Paul and Gail spun round. It was Scott and Lucy from across the courtyard.

'We had bets on this!' called out Lucy.

'What do you mean?'

'Who was going to kiss who first, of course! My bet was on you, Paul. And Scott's was on Gail.'

'Then you're both wrong,' replied her husband.

Their lips met at exactly the same time. It felt the most natural thing to do in the world – as though they'd been kissing each other all their lives!

'To a new beginning,' breathed Paul as they drew apart.

'To a new beginning,' she echoed.

And then their lips met again. After all, they had a lot of loving to make up for …

A Country Practice: New Beginnings
by Judith Colquhoun

A heart-warming and engaging tale, based on the award-winning, Australian television serial *A Country Practice*.

Brendan and Molly Jones swap city living for a new start in the country. But are they prepared for rural life in Wandin Valley?

A Country Practice follows the dramas, loves, secrets and dilemmas of the people in a small country town in south-eastern Australia. There is romance, humour and tragedy for the medical staff and patients of the Wandin Valley Bush Nursing Hospital, and their friends and neighbours.

Brendan and Molly meet the colourful characters who will change their lives forever.

Terence Elliott is the town's respected doctor, but can he overcome his demons to save a mother and baby in danger?

Simon Bowen, the newest doctor in town, is frustrated at being seen as an outsider by the tight knit country people. Will he succeed in winning them around – especially young vet Vicky Dean?

Police sergeant Frank Gilroy has his heart set on Vicky's mum, Sister Shirley Dean. But is he the man for her?

Meanwhile, a teenager in love clashes with her father and a serious car accident reveals a surprising secret about two of the town's residents.

Available exclusively from Amazon

Do You Take This Man?
by Sophie King

**One bride, two choices. What if Katie got married …
and what if she didn't?**

Have you ever wondered 'what if …' you had made a
different decision in life? Would another choice have
taken you down a totally different path? Would life have
been better or worse? Would you have ended up with
someone different?

In *Do You Take This Man?* we follow Katie's two lives
and find out what happens to her if she says 'I do' and
what happens if she stands up her groom.

In many ways, Katie's two separate realities couldn't be
further apart. But we also see how there are some people
and situations you can't avoid, and that perhaps some
things are meant to happen whatever choices you make
in life.

In the tradition of the classic film *Sliding Doors*, *Do You
Take This Man?* is a gripping page turner that will keep
you guessing to the end!

Available exclusively from Amazon

27650994R00141

Printed in Poland
by Amazon Fulfillment
Poland Sp. z o.o., Wrocław